ALYCIA JONES

# Because I was born

First edition

ISBN (paperback): 979-8-9917820-0-5
ISBN (hardcover): 979-8-9917820-1-2

Cover art by Onur B

This book was professionally typeset on Reedsy.
Find out more at reedsy.com

*To my Mom and Dad*
*To my Auntie Vee in Heaven*
*The greatest supporters in my life*
*I love you*

# Acknowledgments

I want to start by thanking God for giving me the strength and courage to complete this project. Without His guidance, none of this would have been possible.

To everyone who has supported me along this journey—thank you. Your encouragement means the world to me. And to those who will purchase this book, I am deeply grateful. This is my first book, and I am incredibly proud of it. The joy of finally achieving something I've worked toward for so long is indescribable.

A special thank you to Paris, the first person to read this book from beginning to end. Your unwavering support and love have been invaluable. Thank you for pushing me forward, even when I felt like giving up.

To my wonderful friend Kyara—your talent, feedback, and support have been instrumental in guiding me through this process. I cannot thank you enough.

Thank you to my Mom for your endless ideas and countless pieces of advice on how to make this story even better. Your wisdom has been a cornerstone in this journey.

To my brother Marquise and sister Carol—thank you for listening to my wild ideas and for always cheering me on. Your contributions and enthusiasm have been so encouraging.

Lastly, thank you to my cover design artist, Onur, for bringing my vision to life. Your creativity has perfectly captured the essence of this book.

I hope that you all find as much joy in reading this book as I did in writing it, and that you fall in love with the story line and characters just as I have.

# Chapter 1

Dark clouds started to fill the sky as I stared upon them. Listening to the sounds of the waves washing up and down the shore, I looked around and took a deep breath. No one around, just me and my thoughts. This is what peace felt like.

I looked down at the watch on my wrist to look at the time. I sighed in frustration as I realized it was time for me to head home. I got up from the warm, humid sand and started to make my way back.

My mom and I use to walk up and down this beach every night just to clear our heads. Hands attached together we would sing songs and discuss our day as we skipped along the shore. I looked forward to the evening walks with her every day. Always cracking jokes making me laugh, she was my best friend.

But lately, everything's changed.

I remember one particular evening; I was getting ready for the daily walk with mom. Being the happy 6-year-old that I was, I rushed to put on my shoes. I was so full of excitement to tell my mom how my day was that I put my shoes on the wrong foot. Noticing by the funny feeling in my toes, I giggled as I quickly changed them. Smiling as I fixed my shoes I got up and headed downstairs.

Stopping in the middle of the stair way I spotted my mom crying. Papa was in front of her with his hand up. I grew curious as I continued to walk down the stairs slowly. Papa had a weird look on his face, kind of

1

like the time when I accidentally spilled juice on his favorite t-shirt. He was not very happy with me that day.

My eyes never leaving my mama and papa, I made it downstairs.

"Mommy? Papa?" I spoke. Their eyes turned to me as my papa lowered his hand. Mommy immediately got up and ran to me. She knelt down on one knee and began to stare into my eyes. She had a look of defeat written all over her face.

"What's wrong mommy?" I asked worriedly. I was worried but also very confused. Mommy and Papa never got upset with each other like this before.

Wiping the tears from her eyes, she gave me a soft smile.

"Nothing baby girl. Are you ready to go for our walk?" she asked and I gently nodded my head.

"Okay"

She looked down at my shoes and smiled.

"You put them on the right foot this time" she whispered.

I looked over my mom's shoulder and seen my dad sitting at the table with his head in his hands.

"What's wrong with papa?" I asked.

My mom looked behind her then back at me, then behind her again, then right back at me and smiled.

"Papa's just tired,"

"Why don't you go get cookie, I think we should take her on a walk with us today" she said.

Giving one last look at my dad, I ran back upstairs to get my dog cookie. I got cookie for my birthday this year, she's a little white scruffy looking dog with patches of brown spots on her body. The best gift ever.

"Cookie" I called as I reached my room.

"Cookie,"

Cookie was always hiding from us. Sometimes I think she's scared of us, or more importantly scared of them.

"Oh cookie!"

I sighed as I continued to look for cookie. I don't think cookie can hear very well.

"Cookie" I said for the last time.

Cookie came out of her hiding place and ran to me. Her tail was wagging as fast as ever as she jumped up onto my legs.

"There you are you silly dog"

"Come on we're going for a walk" I exclaimed.

I grabbed cookie's leash, attached it onto her collar and headed back downstairs.

"I'm sick of this" I heard papa yell and soon there was a huge door being slammed. I jumped from the intensity of the sound. I could feel the stairwell shake a little as the door closed. I felt cookie's warm fur against my leg and I looked down to see her burying her head behind me. I reassured her everything was okay by softly petting her.

I then looked over at mama who was on the ground shaking and crying. I ran over to her and knelt down. "Mamma?"

"Mamma, are you okay?" I asked. She sat up slowly and wiped a little spot of redness off her face.

"I'm fine" she said getting up off the floor. She walked towards the mirror that we had on the wall next to the front door. It was a brown old mirror that had so many different scratches and cracks in it. I'm surprised it hasn't broken yet.

She looked into the mirror and at the now visible scratch on her cheek. She sighed as she held her face.

"Mama will just be one second then we can go for our walk okay?" she said giving a soft smile.

I nodded my head as she walked away and into her bedroom. I walked to the window and looked out of it. I see papa getting into his car and driving off. Something just felt wrong. Papa always gives me a kiss goodbye when he leaves for the day.

Mama came out with suitcases in her hand. "You ready?" She asked me and I looked at her with confusion.

"How come you have bags mama?" I asked.

"I thought you, Cookie and me can get away for a while" she said.

"What about papa?"

"Papa is going to be okay. He's going to have a vacation of his own" she explained calmly.

"Okay." I was confused, I didn't understand how papa could have a vacation without us, without... me.

Mama, Cookie and I walked out of the house and mama put the bags into the car.

"Okay let's take a quick walk then we have to go, okay?"

I nodded in response and held onto Cookie's leash as mama grabbed my hand. We walked to the beach which was just a few steps away from our house, and we started talking.

"So how was your day?" mama asked me. I can hear the tremble in her voice as she was obviously holding in her tears.

"Good, I made a snowman out of clay today at school!" I smiled remembering the fun day that I had at school earlier.

"Really? That's so cool bean!" I love when she calls me bean. Daddy came up with that nickname for me because ever since I could eat real food, I've loved beans. Any kind of bean you can think of, I'll eat it!

We made it close to the water when we decided to sit. I placed cookie onto my lap and started petting her as mama started to stroke my hair.

"Caitlyn?" Mama said to me.

"Yes mama?"

"I want you to know that no matter what happens in life, always be strong. You need to remember that everything happens for a reason and that sometimes things aren't meant to be." she explained.

I was confused and didn't know what she was talking about at all, but all I could do was nod and say, "Okay, Mama." She kissed my forehead and gave me a tight hug. I was only six, but I could feel the pain inside her with just a single touch.

Little did I know that in the future, things wouldn't be meant to be.

Now here I am, 10 years later, and I can still remember that day like it was yesterday. The tears in my mom's eyes and the look on my daddy's face. The way the fur on Cookie's body rose and the way her tail hung low that whole day. Cookie passed away about three years ago. She got hit by a car. I don't think I've ever cried that much before.

I'm not sure what really happened to Dad after everything went down. Mom just says he disappeared, and I shouldn't worry. I'm old enough now to know that's not exactly true. I know that he left. He left us alone. He left... me. I tried to look him up a few times, but there's nothing on him. I don't ask questions because when I do, it's only followed by a lecture from a mad mom.

Yes, a mad mom—that's the word. You'd think after Dad left, I'd still have Mom to count on, but the truth is, I seemed to have lost two parents that day.

"Where have you been?" Mom asked, holding a glass of wine as I entered the house.

"At the beach." I replied blankly.

"Why were you out so late?" she asked bluntly.

"I didn't know 6 o'clock was late." I sassed, starting to walk away. I didn't have the energy for a screaming match with her tonight.

"Listen, Missy, do not talk to me like that. I was just worried about you," she said.

"Okay."

"Can I go to my room now?" I questioned.

"No, you can go clean the kitchen." she asserted.

Sighing as I walked to the kitchen and saw all the dishes in the sink, I started cleaning. This is a never-ending cycle in this household—Mom lays on the couch drinking while I do all the housework. Every day, nothing new. I'm used to it now.

After cleaning for at least an hour, I was exhausted. I turned off the kitchen light and headed upstairs.

"Caitlyn," my mom called out to me from her bedroom.

You've got to be kidding me.

I dragged my feet into her room to see what she wanted.

"Yes?" I answered.

"Can you give your sister a bath?" she asked. Normally, I wouldn't have any problem with bathing my sister, but at this moment, I was super tired.

"Sure," I said as I turned around and walked into my sister's room.

"Hey, little one," I said, looking down at my 3-year-old sister, who was in her bed watching TV.

"Cait," she responded cheerfully.

"You ready for a bath?" I asked.

"No bath."

"Yes bath."

"No bath!"

"Yes bath," I said as I went over to her and started tickling her.

"Don't want to be a smelly girl now, do we?" I said, continuing to tickle her.

"Okay," she laughed. I picked her up and took her into the bathroom. Undressing her and putting her in, I stared at her while she laughed and splashed in the water.

The day my mom told me she was pregnant with her wicked boyfriend's baby was the day my life changed. Not only because I wouldn't be the only child anymore, but because my mom was having a baby with someone I couldn't stand. Someone I will never trust. Ever.

Three and a half years ago, on August 14, my mom came home with Steve, her boyfriend.

"Hey, sweetie, I have some exciting news for you," my mom said.

"You're breaking up?" I asked, and my mom shot me a glare.

"No, we are actually having a baby," she screamed with excitement as I just stared at the ground.

"Come on, aren't you excited?" Steve asked, rubbing my shoulder, as chills spread throughout my body. His hands against my skin felt as if I had just gotten stabbed with a safety pin. Yes, a safety pin.

"Please don't touch me," I said as I shrugged his hand off of me.

"Now, Caitlyn, don't be rude," Mom stated. She was always defending him, in any situation.

"It's fine, Cindy," he said to my mom. "She just has to get used to me," he smirked. I gave him a look of disgust. I didn't like him whatsoever.

"Anyway, isn't this great? You'll have someone to play with," my mom smiled. Is she serious? What am I, five?

"I don't need anyone to play with," I spat.

"Caitlyn, don't be like this," Steve said.

I looked up at him with anger. "Don't talk to me." Who does he think he is?

"Caitlyn," Mom warned.

I got up and started heading to my room. "Wait," Mom said, stopping me. "Come here," she demanded.

I walked slowly back over to her and Steve. "This is an amazing thing. God is giving me another baby. You should be happy. You're going to love this baby." she said softly, grabbing my hand.

"I'm not!" I yelled, yanking my hand back. "I'm not going to love it. I don't care what anyone says—now leave me alone." I yelled, walking away.

I was heartbroken and full of anger. No one asked how I would feel about this. And how does my mom think she can raise another baby when she doesn't even do a good job with me? Yes, I know she's my mother, and maybe I sound like a brat, but it's true.

I didn't want a little sister or brother. I didn't want anything but to be alone.

Those same thoughts stuck with me until the day my little sister was born.

It was my birthday, and I had just turned thirteen when Mom was rushed to the hospital. "Wow, this is great. I have to share my birthday with the thing." I said, annoyed, as I stared out the window of the hospital room.

"Caitlyn, stop." Steve said. I rolled my eyes and kept staring out the window. Mom had just given birth, and we were now waiting for the doctor to bring in the baby.

They soon came in with a little baby the size of a watermelon and handed her to my mom.

I could see my mom's eyes light up as she looked into the baby's eyes. I hadn't seen my mom smile so big in years. Maybe her having this baby is a good thing.

No, no it's not.

She then looked up at me. "Do you want to hold her?" she asked.

No, I do not want to hold this thing.

I hesitated for a while before getting up and walking over to the hospital bed. I sat down, and Steve grabbed the baby and put her into my arms. Immediately, my heart started pounding as I looked at this tiny little baby that my mom had brought into this world.

Oh, I think I changed my mind.

I stared at her for a while, her cute little nose and her little patch of dark brown hair. She began to open her eyes, and butterflies began to take over my stomach.

What is this feeling?

"She opened her eyes," the doctor said.

What does that mean?

"You know, they say the first person the baby sees is going to be the person they are closest to—besides the mom, of course," he said, and I couldn't help but smile.

That's so not true.

I then felt something inside that I hadn't felt in so long—I felt happiness.

The baby began to make a noise, and I jumped back.

"Okay, grab it." I said as the doctor and my mom laughed.

"It's okay; she's just saying hi," the doctor said as he let out another small laugh.

"Have we thought about a name yet?" the doctor asked my mom, and I looked up at her. I hadn't heard any name suggestions because, truthfully, I didn't care to hear them, but now I couldn't wait to hear what was chosen for this beautiful little human.

"Yes," Steve said.

"Claire," my mom answered. Claire was such a beautiful name.

Claire means light or bright, and that's exactly what she was—a light in such a dark time.

"Hi, Claire," I said softly. "I'm your sister."

To this day, I always kiss Claire and tell her I love her. Watching her as she continues to splash in the water, I think, how could I have ever said I wouldn't love this thing?

She's the greatest thing that has happened to me in a while

# Chapter 2

I sat in the front of the class waiting for class to start. I hate this school and everybody in it, except for one person of course, my best friend, Callie. She's been my best friend for years now, we met when we were about 8 years old.

The first time I saw Callie was when her and her family had just moved in down the street from me. My mom had just yelled at me for spilling grape juice on the carpet. I remember me trying to wipe it up with some tissue but all it did was dissolve and make things worse, a disgrace is what my mother called me.

Mom threw me outside after that, she said she couldn't bare to look at me anymore for the day. I was used to it by then though, it was a routine, mom comes home with a strong twisted aroma, I do something to set her off then boom I get punished. I mean, every day it was a different punishment, I would always catch myself wondering what the punishment would be like today. Mom's a creative person, because boy did she come up with some original punishments for me.

I can recall myself sitting outside for hours, when a blue car followed by a huge red and white truck drove by my house. I watched as they drove past my quiet, tree-lined street, the kind where no one usually passes through unless they live here. I got up intrigued as I stared at both vehicles as it began to slow down and turn into a driveway a couple of houses down from me. Curious to see who was moving in, I started to walk closer to the house, I wasn't supposed to leave my house but, I knew mom wouldn't care to check up on me anyway.

The back-car door of the blue sedan opened as I seen two feet about the same size of mine plop to the ground. A little girl then got out of the car and all I can think about was how pretty she looked, with her long curly brown hair, her glowing caramel brown skin, and baby blue eyes. She had a different persona than I've seen in a while, she just seemed so bubbly and happy.

She then looked up at me and I turned away quick embarrassed that she had caught me staring. I started to walk back to my house when I was stopped by a touch on my shoulder. I turned around and there she was, right in my face.

"Hi!" she stated cheerfully as she cheesed from ear to ear.

"Oh uh- hi." I stuttered as I smiled back.

"What's your name?" she asked,

"Caitlyn".

"Caitlyn? That's such a pretty name!" she said, and I blushed.

"Thanks." I replied softly.

"I'm 8, how old are you?" she asked me.

"Me too." I said. She then stopped smiling as she looked me deep into the eyes. Is she trying to cast a spell on me? Why is she just staring?

"Are you okay?" she asked, and my heart sank.

"Yes." I said nodding my head up and down. She then shook her head.

"Something is wrong" she said, I was so confused as to how she could tell something was wrong. She doesn't even know me.

"No, I'm fine." I lied. She then began to observe me. She looked me up and down, and all around. I felt like I was at a check up at the doctors or something.

"What's this?" she asked pointing to a bruise I had on my shoulder.

"Oh, um I had tripped over something and fell and that got there." I lied again. I'm such a bad liar.

She nodded her head, letting the subject go. I looked over her shoulder and seen that a man and woman who must have been her parents looking at us.

"I think you have to go." I said to her as she turned around and seen her parents. She looked back at me and nodded.

"Okay, can I tell you something first?" she asked me, and I nodded.

"You're amazing." was what she said as she started to walk off. I didn't know what it was about her but I just felt safe. At 8 years old, she seemed much more advanced and mature than I could ever be.

I watched her as she headed inside when she turned around one last time.

"Oh yeah, my name is Callie, maybe we can have play dates sometimes?" she yelled while smiling. I gave her a thumbs up as I turned around and headed back to my house.

Callie. Wow.

Little did I know that day was only the beginning to a beautiful friendship and ever since then we've been closer than ever. She was there for me through all the times, good and bad, and I was there for her.

"So, how's everything at home?" Callie asked as she took out her sparkly orange folder from her book bag and sat it on the desk. Callie loved bright colors; she had the brightest personality.

"It could be better." I sighed as I tapped my pencil up and down on the desk.

She gave me a soft smile, "Want to come over today? Mom's making tacos." she said smirking knowing that I love tacos.

I frowned once I realized I couldn't, mom was going out tonight and she never let's me go anywhere when she's out. "I would love to, but I forgot I have to watch Claire while my mom goes out with Steve." I said rolling my eyes at the thought of Steve. No one *really* understands why

I dislike that man with a passion.

"Aw come on Cait give him a chance."

"I tried for nearly 5 years; I can't do it anymore." I said getting annoyed.

"Well maybe—"

"Okay class good morning please take your seats." Ms. Smith, our home room and first period teacher stated as she walked through the door carrying a stack of papers.

"How was everybody's weekend?" She asked looking down at all of her students.

The class began to retort with responses like "to short" or "not long enough". Nobody likes being at this school, they'd rather be at home doing whatever it is that they do, except for me of course.

I mean, don't get me wrong, yes, I do hate this school, but believe it or not, I find it so much better than being home with *those people.*

"What about you Caitlyn? How was your weekend?" Ms. Smith asked me as she gave me an indulgent smile.

I looked up at her anxiously, I hate speaking in front of so many people.

"Um, it was great." I lied smiling uncomfortably. She then gave me a look of uncertainty as if she could tell I was obviously lying. Yeah, I've never been the best liar.

She then just nodded her head as she continued to interact with the students in the classroom.

I looked at Callie and sighed, she knows I was lying as well, I just can't let anyone know what really goes on in my household. Not even Callie knows half of the shit that I encounter at home.

Some time has passed, and Ms. Smith had given us an assignment to do. We were able to work in pairs, so of course I paired up with Callie.

"What were you saying before we were interrupted?" I asked writing both our names on one sheet of paper.

"Oh, I was going to say maybe you can bring Claire with you to my house, I mean if that's okay with your parents." She said and I cringed by the word 'parents'.

"Sure, I'll ask when I get home and let you know."

The day went on and it was lunch time. Surprisingly the food here is pretty good. It's set up to where it's like a little buffet, they have a decent number of choices too.

"Well look who it is, the biggest whore of the school." Spat Josh, a curly headed jerk who absolutely hates my guts. I am without a clue as to why he hates me so much, but I honestly couldn't care less.

"Find some new jokes Josh, that one's getting old." I replied irritated as I got my tray and started to pick from the different variety of foods.

He laughed maliciously,

"You know what *is* getting old?" He asked.

"No, but I'm dying to know." I sarcastically answered.

"Those shoes and that outfit. I mean this is what, the third day in a row that you wore it?" He laughed.

I looked down at myself and instantly started to feel self-conscious. No, I have not worn this outfit for three days in a row, but I do wear it often. It's a comfort outfit of mine. Callie got it for me last year for my birthday and it just makes me happy.

"Ever heard of a washing machine?" Callie jumped in from wherever it was she came from.

"Leave her alone." She strictly added. Josh was unexpectedly scared of Callie for some odd reason. I just think he likes her, which is revolting in every way possible.

Sucking his teeth, Josh walked away.

"Thanks." I softly smiled.

I hated not standing up for myself. I hated when people had to defend me. I hated not being able to take control of my own situation.

"No problem, that boy has no life" Callie spoke reaching for a tray.

We reached the end of the food line and I put in my school identification number to be able to receive the food.

Walking together, looking for an empty table, we finally spotted one and sat down. I stared at Callie as she started to eat her food, I just wasn't in the mood to eat anymore.

"Are you okay?" Callie asked, noticing how I was playing with my food.

I nodded my head in response, not looking up from my food. She put her fork down and wiped her mouth.

"What's wrong? I know somethings wrong."

"Nothing is wrong Callie." I said starting to get a bit aggravated. Callie is the type to keep pushing and pushing until she gets a response out of you. It can be a bit frustrating sometimes. When I get upset I like to just keep quiet for a while until I can gather my thoughts and clear my head.

"Are you sure? You look sad now" She added, but I didn't respond.

"Is it because of Josh?" She continued.

"Come on Cait, you know he's a tweak"

"Callie, I said I'm fine!" I yelled. She looked at me, surprised at my sudden outburst.

"I'm sorry I was just asking." She said in her defense.

"Okay and I told you I'm fine, now can you drop it?!" I shouted. Almost everyone in the entire cafeteria was looking at me. I didn't know what came across me, I just got so angry.

"Fine." She mumbled getting up and moving to a different table. I sighed and rested my head into my hands.

"No actually," Callie stated as she started to walk back towards the table that we were sitting at.

"Why do you always have to take your anger out on me?" She asked.

"It's like you blow up on people who actually care about you, all I'm trying to do is help and you-"

"Maybe I don't want your help Callie, can't you see that?" I interrupted.

"I don't need your pity-"

"Pity? Who said anything about pi-" She started,

"I don't want your pity, and I don't need your sympathy, so if you're just going to continue to do it then stay away from me." I spat.

I can tell she was extremely hurt by what I was saying, and truthfully, I don't even *know* why I was saying all of this. I just exploded for no reason.

"Caitlyn, what are you talking about?" She said sitting back down at the table. "We've been best friends for nearly 8 years, how can you even say this?" She quietly asked.

I felt the tears in my eyes beginning to form. I refuse to let anyone see me cry. No one has ever seen me cry before and I plan on keeping it that way.

"Cait, please just tell me what's wrong. I'm no therapist but I promise you I will listen, and I will care." She pleaded.

Everything is different with Callie; she brings things out of me that I always wish to be kept inside.

"Stop shutting me out, let me in." she added.

I wanted to talk about it, hell, I wanted to scream about it. I wanted to yell, I wanted to shout about it, but all I could do was whisper,

"I'm fine."

# Chapter 3

"Why can't Claire just come with me?" I yelled to my mother who had just told me that I couldn't go to Callie's house because I had to watch Claire. I had just gotten home from school and all I could think about was the conversation that I had with Callie. I needed to talk to her about it because I felt so bad about snapping on her because she's the one person who I can usually go to for peace.

"Because I don't trust you with her when you're with Callie!" My mother lividly yelled back.

"You're acting like I'm going to leave her to get eaten by their dog or something." I rolled my eyes.

Walking away she spat, "Well who knows what you'll do."

This is what makes me mad about my mother. She never trusts me. Ever. Which hurts because I have done nothing to cause her to treat me this way. Besides it's me who takes care of Claire on a daily basis anyway.

"So now what? I have to cancel my plans?" I asked following my infuriating mother around the house.

"You betcha." she stopped and gave me a wicked smile.

"No one told you that you can go over there in the first place." she added as she continued to walk away from me and I followed.

She's so evil I could cry.

"You never had a problem with me going over there before, but now all of a sudden I have to change *my* plans so *you* can go out with your dumb boyfriend." I screamed and was abruptly struck by a slap on my face.

Red with anger, my mother hit me again, this time twice as hard.

"You will NOT talk to me like I'm your friend. I am your mother and what I say goes, you hear?!"

Oh now you're my mother.

I was too mad to say anything, I was really trying to hold in my tears and my anger, I refuse to let her see me weak.

"DO YOU HEAR ME?!?" She screamed again plangently.

"Yes." I softly responded.

She then walked away, and I went into my room slamming my door. She's always ruining my mood and my life. I can never be happy in this house.

Dialing Callie's number, I shed a few tears.

Callie answered the phone in just two rings,

"Hello?" she answered

"Callie I can't come I'm sorry."

"Why not? Are you okay?" She asked in a concerned tone.

I wiped away my tears,

"I'm fine." I lied. "She's not letting me go because she doesn't want Claire over there." Like I suspected.

"Awe, okay well next time." She replied.

"Okay, see you tomorrow." I said before hanging up the phone. I threw the phone on the bed and plopped down on top of it.

I took a few breaths as I tried to calm down. Besides school, Callie's house is the only place where I can run away from my own. I hate being home, this house makes me feel so much that I start to feel nothing, if that makes sense. It's like I'm becoming more numb as days go by.

I touched my still stinging face from the hits, I was surprised she only hit me twice because usually, it's always so much more.

I heard some tiny footsteps that was leading up to my room door, followed by little knocks. I smiled softly knowing that it was Claire coming to check on me. She always checks on me after these *things* happen.

Walking over to the door, I opened it and let Claire in.

"Hey baby." I said looking down at my adorable little sister.

Closing the door behind her, we both made our way to my bed. With the bed being too high for Claire, I gave her a little boost.

"How's it going?" I smiled at her. "Good, how are you?" She replied in her adorable high-pitched voice.

I smiled at her. She's only three years old but she's as smart as a whip. I guess that's just because I teach her everything she needs to know.

"I'm okay." I grinned.

Touching my red face her eyes began to water. She knew what just went down, her lip began to quiver, and I already knew what was about to happen.

"Oh no baby don't cry." I said sympathetically. "I'm okay, I promise." I added.

Poking out her lip she let a few tears drop. I wrapped her into a tight hug and started rocking her. I hate that she has to see this kind of stuff at such a young age. I want better for her; I never want her to go through what I went through. I just want my sister to have a much better life and have fun, like I always wanted to do. Be a kid like I always wanted to be.

Looking up at me with a wet face, "Mommy hurt you again." She spoke. It wasn't a question; it was a statement.

"It's just because sissy didn't be quiet. I was talking too much and wasn't listening to mommy so she..." I paused. I didn't know how to say 'she hit me' to a three-year-old.

"Hurt you." Claire added for me.

I nodded my head in agreement. "Can you listen to mommy please?" She begged.

"I don't want you hurt." she said as her voice started shaking.

"Of course, I'll listen from now on, okay?" I said stroking her hair. She nodded her tiny little head and laid back down on my chest.

*If only she knew the half of it.*

That night Claire and I had a little movie night. She wanted popcorn and skittles, such a weird combination but I made sure she had it.

"Here catch." I said as I took a skittle and threw it up in the air waiting for Claire to catch it with her mouth.

She missed by a long shot and we both started cracking up laughing.

"Almost." I laughed as I took another skittle.

"Okay this time keep your eye on the skittle." I said holding the skittle close to her face and she giggled.

"Remember, eye on the skittle, don't look away." I said as I got ready to throw the skittle up in the air.

Her eyes never leaving the skittle, I threw it up and she made her way over to where it was going to land and caught it.

Shocked that she actually caught it, we both started screaming and jumping up and down.

"I caught it Cait, I caught it!!" She yelled happily. "You did! Good job!" I happily yelled back.

"Again, again!" she cheered and we spent a few minutes throwing and catching the skittles.

For the time being that mom and Steve was out, Claire and I had so much fun giggling and watching movies. I love this little girl so much; she makes me forget about everything that I'm going through.

"How's school going?" I asked Claire who was now munching on the popcorn.

She doesn't go to real school of course, but she does go to a daycare center that teaches her little things here and there.

"It's good." she said but something about the way she said it wasn't convincing.

"You sure?" I asked raising an eyebrow. She started to play with her little fingers. Claire always plays with her fingers when she isn't being honest.

"You can talk to me." I grabbed her hand and held them.

"Ms. Honey doesn't like me." she said looking down.

Ms. Honey is Claire's daycare teacher, a real bitch if you ask me, but my mom can afford her so. I don't get it though. How can anyone not like Claire? She's the cutest, sweetest girl ever.

"What do you mean? How do you know?" I asked.

"When it's time for snacks she always gives the other kids their food first and she leave me with the crummies." She said continuing to look down.

"And she always talks about my clothes and says that they are dirty, and mommy doesn't have money to get new ones". She added.

What kind of teachers tells this to a three-year-old? I felt myself starting to get angry, but I didn't want to say how I was feeling in front of Claire.

Ms honey has some nerves talking about someone's clothes when she comes to work dressed like a giant bumble bee every morning.

I lifted up Claire's chin.

"It's okay, don't listen to what she's saying okay? I'm going to tell mommy so she can fix it alright?" I said trying to get her to feel better.

"Okay." she said.

"I won't let anyone, or anything hurt you, always remember that." I said, and she smiled.

We continued to watch our movie until we heard the knob on the door being turned.

"Mommy's home." I said rolling my eyes. Mom and Steve then walked in the house. My mom was walking all wobbly and Steve was helping her stand up straight.

"Is she D-R-U-N-K?" I spelled out to him and he smiled wickedly.

"Maybe." he smirked. Ugh I wanted to slap him. He knows what my mom does when she's intoxicated.

He then walked her to the couch where Claire and I were sitting, and she fell onto it. I picked up Claire and moved her closer to me.

"Well, have fun." Steve said laughing. "So, you're just going to leave us here with her?" I asked.

"Yep. Bye." he said walking out the door. I couldn't believe this idiot, and where the heck was, he even going, he lives here!

"Hey Caitlynn," my mom slurred. "Go get me a drink." she said with her eyes closed and hand in the air.

"Yeah, I think you've had enough drinks for one night." I said getting up and walking over to my mom to help her up to go to bed.

"Come on let's go to bed." I said grabbing her hand.

"NO!" she shouted. "Don't touch me!" She screamed as she yanked her hand from me.

She then got up quickly and wobbled and almost fell. I caught her before she did fall, and she stood up straight.

"You Missy don't tell me what to do." she continued to slur. "Mom please." I pleaded remembering that Claire was in the room watching.

"Shut the hell up!" she said pushing me and continued to wobble.

"Claire go upstairs." I said to my sister who was looking scared.

She got up and started to go upstairs. "No Claire, stay." my mom demanded.

"Mom please she's tired let her go to sleep." I begged.

"Listen bitch!" She yelled and my eyes widened. "I said don't tell me what to do!" She said as she grabbed her purse and whacked me across my face with it.

I held my face because whatever she had in her purse hurt beyond measures. The only thing I can think about was that Claire was watching.

"Claire go upstairs now!" I yelled

"No Claire!" Mom yelled back. Claire was stuck, she didn't know what to do. She then began to cry loud.

I walked over to her and picked her up and headed upstairs. "You get back here you punk!" mom said as she followed us walking unsteadily.

I raced upstairs with Claire in my arms and went inside her room.

"Cait I'm scared." she cried. "Shh." I cooed.

"It's okay mommy's not feeling well she'll be fine." I said.

We then heard a loud bang as my mom had kicked the door open. Standing in the doorway with a broom stick, Claire started to scream of terror.

I placed Claire on the bed and stood in front of her while my mom got in front of me.

"Mommy please, please calm down!" I croaked out.

"Don't tell me to calm down!" She said as she hit the nearest lamp with the broom stick and broke it. All I can hear was Claire screaming.

"You are just-" she said as she hit the other lamp.

"Like-" She hit the TV.

"Your fucking- "she hit the desk

"Father!" She screamed hitting the door causing it to break.

"Always telling me what to do!" She yelled as she threw the broom stick down in front of me.

My breathing picked up; I have seen my mother act somewhat crazy when she was drunk but never like this.

"Its always my fault right? Never anyone else." She yelled.

"Okay I'm sorry." I spoke.

"Come here Claire!" She yelled for Claire to come.

"Why? What do you want with her?" I asked. My mother picked back up the broom stick and held it up like she was about to hit me.

"I said come here!" She shrieked. Claire got up from her bed slowly. I didn't know what to do, I thought if I held her back it would make things worse, so I let her go.

Claire finally got down from her bed and my mom dragged her by her shirt. Claire screamed, clearly terrified of my raging mother.

My mom then began to hit Claire with the broom stick.

"This is for not listening to me!" She yelled hitting her repeatedly.

Claire winced in pain and cried her eyes out.

"Mom stop!" I yelled to my mother as I tried to stop her from beating Claire.

"You better step away or you're going to get it even harder!" my mother said to me.

"Okay that's fine, hit me, do whatever just don't hurt Claire. She didn't do anything wrong please." I literally begged.

"Please!" I said again louder but my mom continued.

"Mommy please she's just a baby!" I cried.

My mom then stopped and there it was, the quick mood change began to show as she dropped down to her knees and started crying.

I immediately grabbed Claire and picked her up. She was sobbing uncontrollably, and her heart was racing.

I looked at my mother who was still on the floor sobbing herself. I couldn't handle this, I just wanted to break down myself, but I had to be the strong one.

As much as I wanted to see my mom in pain for what she did, I couldn't. She's my mother and no matter what she does I always find a way to forgive her.

"It's okay Claire just breathe, match my breathing." I said as I took deep breaths indicating for Claire to copy me.

I looked at my baby sister who was devastated. There were marks on her arm and legs from the broom. I felt the tears swelling up in my eyes, but I refuse to cry.

My mother got up and both Claire and I tensed up. We thought she was going to hit us again but instead she simply just walked out.

Claire started to cry again.

"Claire please calm down, I promise you it's okay." I said holding her face into my hands.

"You s-said that" she started but paused because of all the crying she was doing.

"What did I say?" I asked. She continued to weep.

"You said that you wouldn't let anyone hurt me." She cried and my heart broke. I didn't even know what to say, I did promise her that no one would hurt her, and her own mother did.

"I know, I'm sorry, mommy isn't well we have to help her." I explained and she shook her head.

"I'm scared." She whispered.

"I know." I said quietly.

Me too.

# Chapter 4

The next morning, I woke up feeling emotionally and mentally debilitated. I was drained after what took place last night, I mean, who wouldn't be? Claire ended up sleeping in my room because she was afraid to go back to hers, which was fine with me because I honestly felt the exact same way.

I stared at my baby sister as she slept peacefully with her arms wrapped around me. Tear stains still on her face, and her hair a mess, she was still the most beautiful little girl ever. I promised her I wouldn't ever let anyone hurt her and in just a matter of minutes I completely broke my promise.

This isn't how life is supposed to be, I'm not supposed to be trying to protect my sister from the woman who birthed her. The woman who out of everyone is supposed to be the one person that she can go to for anything. The woman who is supposed to make sure that her and I both feel safe at all times. Instead, she's the woman that we fear.

I'm not supposed to be crying every day and night feeling alone, feeling like no matter what I do there's always going to be that one thing that breaks me down in the end. That one thing is my mother. What is the purpose of living in pain every day? Not physically, but mentally, is there a point?

Claire started to squirm around in the bed indicating that she was beginning to wake up. I watched her as she opened her eyes and began to wipe the crust out of them.

"Good morning sleepy head." I smiled. All I could do was hope and pray that she would somehow forget about what happened last night, but even God himself couldn't make that happen in this moment.

"Mommy here?" She asked as she began to look around.

"I'm not sure baby, do you want me to go check?" I questioned and she shook her head.

"Stay." she said as she held onto my hand as tight as she could. She was scared and it made me really sad.

I sat down with Claire in my bed watching TV for about an hour until we both were beginning to get hungry.

I turned the TV off and looked at Claire who was just staring into space. "How about we go get breakfast?" I asked grabbing her face gently so she can look at me. She shook her head, clearly afraid to go outside of my room.

"It'll be okay, mommy isn't going to hurt us again." I said trying to convince myself. She hesitated for a moment before stretching her arms out for me to pick her up.

I grabbed her and opened my bedroom door and headed downstairs to the kitchen. There was mom sitting at the kitchen table drinking a cup of coffee and eating toast. I can feel the heartbeat of Claire against my chest began to speed up as we entered the kitchen.

"It's okay." I whispered in her ear.

"Good morning." I said to my mom who just looked up and ignored me.

I took a deep breath before putting Claire down so I can fix her something to eat. Claire held on to my leg and stuck to me like glue.

I opened the fridge and started searching for some food, but the fridge was as empty as mom's soul.

"We ain't got no food so I don't know what you're looking for." said my mom as she finally turned her attention towards me. I closed the fridge and let out a sigh.

"Claire needs something to eat, she's hungry." I stated as my mom looked at me like I was dumb.

"Then go get some food then." she replied bluntly. I didn't have the time or energy to argue with her this morning and I definitely didn't want a repeat of last night.

"Okay." I said as I grabbed Claire and started to walk back to my room.

"Hold up wait!" My mom said stopping me.

"Leave Claire with me." she said, my stomach sank. I can tell that Claire was about to freak out with the way she was looking.

"Hurry up dammit I ain't going to hurt the child" she yelled. She wasn't intoxicated anymore but I still didn't want to leave her with her, but I knew if I didn't, things would turn left.

I put Claire down and knelt to her level. "Okay baby you're going to stay with mommy for a little bit, okay?" I started and Claire eyes began to water as she shook her head repeatedly.

"No, no, no." she cried.

"Shh, shh, it's going to be okay, okay? I will be back as soon as possible with some yummy food. I'll bring you some more skittles too! You'll be fine, I promise." I told her and she began to calm down. She gave me a big hug and I couldn't help but start to tear up.

"I'll be back." I said one last time. I grabbed her hand and walked her to my mom who was now in the living room on the couch watching her adult channel.

"Do you think you can turn to the cartoons?" I asked her and she rolled her eyes turning to cartoons and motioned for me to go away.

I sighed as I went upstairs to get ready to walk to the store. I hated going to the store alone, so I called Callie to see if she wanted to come with me. We usually walk to the store every day after school, the snack store is Callie's favorite place.

Callie ended up saying yes, so I got ready and headed out. Callie only lived a few houses down from me, so we met up with each other fairly quickly.

"Hey girl!" she said all jolly and happy. Sometimes I envy how joyful she is, I just wish I can be that happy.

"Hey." I replied. "Look I'm sorry again for that conversation we had at school yesterday, I'm not sure what came over me." I apologized as we headed to our local grocery store.

"Cait, it's okay" she giggled. "Trust me I've learned to deal with your little mood swings." she said and we both cracked up laughing.

We continued to walk in comfortable silence for a few minutes, just enjoying the scenery. I lived in a great neighborhood, there were always people doing their daily walks or kids riding their bikes. It's always nice to walk and see everyone living their life being so happy and free.

"So, was everything okay last night? You sounded really out of it when you called." Callie asked breaking the silence as we stopped to look both ways before crossing the street.

"Um, yeah, I was just really tired and upset that I couldn't go to your house." I replied as she raised an eyebrow.

"Did anything else happen?" She asked concerned.

"No, what makes you think anything else happened?" I asked as we finally crossed the street.

"Well, your face kind of looks bruised." She said and my heart dropped as flashbacks from last night popped up in my head. Why didn't I think to try to cover this up?!

"Cait, you don't have to try to hide things from me, I'm your best friend you can trust me." She said stopping me from walking so we can look each other in the eye.

"I know Callie, it's just..."

"It's just what?" She asked and I felt the tears began to form. No Caitlyn you are not crying today, you are not!

"It's just embarrassing." I said still refusing to let the tears fall.

"It's so embarrassing having to tell people that your own mom is constantly drunk, constantly talking down on you and constantly acting like your enemy." I said as my voice began to shake.

"I used to have a mother Callie, a mother that was my best friend. We did everything together we told each other everything. There wasn't a care in the world that I had because I knew mommy would be there for me regardless. Now, it's like I don't even know who she is anymore! She doesn't talk to me unless it's to yell at me for not cleaning or demanding me to grab her a beer. She doesn't look me in the eye anymore Callie. She doesn't love me anymore! Why doesn't she love me? Why doesn't anyone love me?" I screamed. I closed my eyes because I felt myself beginning to cry and I couldn't let that happen.

It's a lot. No one wants to feel as if they don't matter to anyone especially the woman who gave birth to them.

"Caitlyn," Callie said as she grabbed my hands. I opened my eyes and Callie looked into them.

"I love you! I love you so much. You're worth everything. It's okay you don't have to be embarrassed with me. Okay? No, I don't understand exactly what you're going through but I'm always here for you no matter what. Your mom loves you; she's just going through a time right now and the only thing she needs right now is you to help her." She explained sympathetically.

"I know it's hard, I know you can feel alone sometimes but always remember, you have people. Like Claire, I see how she looks at you, she looks at you for comfort, for support, for laughter, for happiness. You give her happiness; you give me happiness. You are worth everything. Never forget that."

I began to calm down as I took a deep breath. "Thank you" I said to Callie. "Come here." she said as she embraced me in a hug. We were legit standing in the middle of the street hugging until a car decided to hunk and ruin our little moment.

Callie flipped them off as we continued to head back to the store laughing our heads off.

# Chapter 5

"Regular or sour?" Callie said holding up two packs of skittles for me to choose for Claire. We had been in the store for about fifteen minutes now, picking up pretty much everything we see.

"Regular, I don't think Claire will be able to handle the sourness." I laughed. Callie put the skittles into the cart, and we continued with our shopping journey.

"What do you think I should do about my mom?" I asked Callie who was looking at snack cakes as if she had just seen the love of her life walk pass. "I think you should tell her how you're feeling about everything." She said, her eyes never leaving the snack cakes.

"This is my mom we're talking about; she can barely say hello to me when she sees me, let alone sit and listen to what I have to say about what I feel *she's* doing wrong."

"You're just going to have to make her Caitlyn, it's not right that's she's doing all of this to you and Claire, anyone who isn't me would have called Protective Services already." Callie said grabbing three boxes of Twinkies and throwing it in the cart. Callie is the size of a twig, but she eats as if her stomach is the size of a whale.

"You're right." I sighed as we finally headed to the register to check out.  I looked at our cart that was filled with food that'll hurt our stomachs and rot our teeth and sighed. What was I thinking? I don't have enough money for this stuff.

"I got you Cait." Callie said placing the groceries on the conveyor belt. She knew exactly what I was thinking, it was like she could legit read my mind at times.

"No Callie, I got it." I stated, knowing for a fact that I didn't have it. I couldn't let her know that though, even though it's clear she sorts of already does.

"Come on Cait, you've done so much for me, let me do this one little thing." She pleaded as she pulled out her debit card and inserted it into the payment terminal.

"But-" I started as I heard the sound of the transaction going through.

"Oops already done." she said as she stuck her tongue out and giggled. I rolled my eyes playfully as I started to put the groceries in the bag.

"Thanks so much seriously."

"It's seriously no problem, most of these are mine anyway, but anything for you." she said laughing while grabbing some grocery bags. I grabbed the other half of the bags and we started to head out.

*Breaking News*

Two words that will catch everyone's attention, just blasted on the TV. I looked up at the TV monitor that was in front of the store, it was on the news channel and a reporter had just popped up.

*"Something is going to happen."*

*"Something strange is going to happen."*

Wait what? I was confused, what was going to happen and why is nobody panicking right now?

"Callie did you hear that?" I asked Callie who had already opened a box of Twinkies and was now stuffing her face.

"Hear what?" she said with a mouthful of vanilla creamy grossness.

"A reporter came on the TV and said that something strange is going to happen." I tried explaining to her, but she was too deep into her

Twinkie to focus.

"Really?" Callie said seeming very uninterested. I looked around to see if anyone else was watching the TV. I saw an older woman who was sitting staring at the TV, I wanted to know if she had heard it as well, so I decided to go ask.

"Hello," I said as I slowly walked up to the lady. The lady slowly looked at me and stared, weirdly, chills took over my arms.

"Um, I was wondering if you happened to know what the reporter said on the TV?" I asked timidly. The lady stared at me for a few more seconds before returning her attention back to the TV without saying a word. Okay?

"Caitlyn what are you doing?" Callie said walking up to me with cream all over her mouth.

"I wanted to know if anyone else heard the reporter on the TV, it's kind of weird." I said wiping the cream off the side of her mouth.

"Oh thanks" she giggled. "I still have no clue what you're talking about though." she said.

"Never mind, maybe I was just hearing things."

"Come on we should head back now." I continued, and we started to walk out. I'm not sure what was happening, but I felt really weird all of a sudden. I know for a fact that I heard that reporter clearly. And the old lady, why did she just ignore me? Could she not speak? Hear? I don't know.

Callie and I made it to the store exit, and we walked out. I looked up and the sky had turned a dark Grey, as if a big storm was coming.

"I think it's about to rain, we should hurry up." I said to Callie who was texting on her phone. There were much more cars on the road and people outside than when we first left. You ever have that bizarre feeling that sits in the pit of your stomach when you feel like something bad is about to happen? Well, that is how I'm feeling right about now.

Callie put down her phone for a split second as we crossed the street only to pick it back up again.

Suddenly I felt a big gust of wind hit me, confusion started to take over my body as I looked around trying to see what was going on. Everything was foggy, everything was a blur. I felt my hands start to tremble and all I could hear was the sound of strong wind. It sounded like a monster in some raggedy cartoon. It then felt as if everything was going in slow motion, I felt like I couldn't breathe. I tried to turn around towards Callie, but it was like my body weight was as heavy as wooden bricks. Panicking, I closed my eyes and took deep breaths trying to calm myself down. Maybe I'm just having a severe panic attack. I kept my eyes closed, then unexpectedly it stopped. It was quiet as a mouse, everything and everyone was frozen, everything that is, except for me.

My body weight wasn't heavy anymore, so I was able to move around and the fog was gone so I was able to see. I turned towards Callie who was frozen solid, in the same position she was in, texting.

"Callie!" I screamed. I could hear myself, but my voice was almost like it was very distant. I started to shake Callie, but she didn't even budge. Her body felt cold and stiff, like a metal statue. I started to panic as I looked around, there were people in cars frozen, people walking on the sidewalks frozen! What is going on?

Tears started to form in my eyes, I didn't understand what was happening, I have to be dreaming this can't be happening. I need to wake up! Wake up Caitlyn! Wake up!

Still in complete panic mode I took out my phone. I tried calling my mom but as soon as I dialed the number my phone froze. I looked around again, while my breath started to pick up, my eyes landed on something. It was a guy in a blue pick-up truck who had a big scratch with blood on his face and his head was resting on the steering wheel. I don't know why but something drew me to that truck. Curiously, I started to walk closer to the truck which had a huge fresh dent in the front, almost like the man had just been in a wreck.

As I got closer to the truck, the sound of that strong wind started to come back again. The anxiety in my body began to pick up as that big gust of wind hit me once again. Shaking, I tried to keep my eyes open this time, everything was spinning in circles and I felt like I was going to pass out. It felt like some extreme roller coaster at the amusement park, only faster. I fought to keep my eyes open to see what was happening, and there it was. The man who was in the truck was driving by fast, going beyond the speed limit. He had loud music blasting and talking on the phone. Still being nearly blown away by the wind I kept my eyes on the truck. People around us were still frozen, everything was frozen except for me and the guy in the truck. Still going super-fast, not paying attention to the road, the truck started to swerve.

I can see the guy starting to panic as he notices his front tire blew out. The truck still swerving around, he tries to control it. Next thing you know the wind gets stronger and now I am unable to see anything. All I can hear is the sound of the strong wind followed by a big crash sound.

I gave up and closed my eyes trying to relax, but the wind was now as strong as ever. I took a deep breath and then it finally stopped.

"Caitlyn are you okay?" I heard Callie say. Realizing my eyes were still closed I opened them and looked around. Everything was normal, the sky wasn't Grey anymore and nobody was frozen. I turned around and seen Callie staring at me in concern, I walked to her and gave her a big hug. My heart was rapidly beating, and my anxiety was a wreck.

"Are you okay? What's wrong?' Callie asked more worried than ever. I tried to control my breathing so I can explain but it wouldn't work.

"Cait, just breathe." Callie said. "Follow my breathing." she said as she did breathing techniques for me to follow. I followed her breathing, and I began to relax.

"Now what happened?" She asked again. "You-you, everything was-, the truck-, the scratch-, the wind." I stuttered, I couldn't even talk. Callie looked at me strange. Did she not just see any of this? Did *nobody* see what just happened?

"Caitlyn, I think we should take you home, I think you need a nap." She said as she grabbed my hand. The grocery bags were still hooked onto my wrist as if nothing happened.

"Okay." I choked out nodding my head. We started to walk and then suddenly I heard loud music starting to come in from the distance. I turned towards the direction of the music and then seen the same exact blue pick-up truck that I had seen before. My heart dropped and my stomach sank, there is no way that that's the same guy, it can't be.

I stared at the truck as it was about to drive pass us and I waited to see the driver. The truck approached us and there he was, the same man that I had previously saw before, except there was no scratch nor dent in his truck.

"Callie!' I yelled. "Callie the truck!" I continued to yell as I sprinted off trying to chase the fast truck.

"Caitlyn what are you doing?!" Callie yelled from behind me. I had to stop the truck; something was telling me to stop it. I continued running towards the truck screaming for people to help me stop it.

"Stop that truck please!" I screamed repeatedly. I then heard a loud pop as I noticed his front tire blew. I stopped running as I see the truck begin to swerve. No.

The truck driver had tried to step on the brakes, but he was going so fast that the car flipped over. The truck flipped in slow motion and all I could do was stand there. I was completely shocked; this is the same exact thing that I had just seen. Was this the strange thing the reporter was talking about? Am I going crazy? Yes, I am definitely going crazy.

"Caitlyn!" Callie yelled as she pulled me back from being too close to the truck. The truck had stopped flipping and landed right back on the wheels. I looked at the truck driver and saw that same scratch and that same dent on the truck. I couldn't believe what I was witnessing, and the scary part is, I've already witnessed it.

# Chapter 6

"**A**re you sure you're okay?" Callie asked as we both walked into my front door. I was loss for words. I couldn't believe what I just saw.

"Callie," I swallowed,

"You're telling me you didn't feel the heavy wind and the spinning, and the shaking, and you didn't see the truck and the man- "

"Cait," Callie said stopping me.

"I saw the accident, yes, but there wasn't any strong wind or anything." Callie said in a confused tone. I started to hyperventilate; I can't be the only one that seen or felt all of that.

"Are you okay? I think you need to take a nap; you've had a long night and morning." Callie said as she grabbed my hand and led me to the living room.

I sat on the couch and took some deep breaths, still shook by what happened when my mom and Claire walked in.

Claire spotted Callie and instantly ran to her and gave her a big hug. Claire loved Callie; they have this little bond and it is the cutest thing ever. Sometimes I think Callie likes to see Claire more than me, and Claire like to see Callie more. It's really adorable.

"Hi little one!" Callie exclaimed while picking up Claire and giving her a big hug. She then put her down and looked to my mom.

"Hi Mrs. Miller" Callie said to my mother who just waved and gave Callie a fake smile.

"What's wrong with you?" My mom spat looking at me as if I was crazy. Maybe I am crazy. Maybe what I saw didn't really happen. Maybe my mind is playing tricks on me. It has to be playing tricks on me.

"Cait." Claire said as she crawled on my lap and stared at me.

"Where's my skittles?" she asked, and I let out a little giggle. Callie reached into the plastic bag that we got from the store and pulled out a pack of red skittles and handed it to Claire.

"Thank you." she smiled hard as she climbed off my lap and ran to the other side of the couch.

"So, did you not hear me? What's wrong with you?" My mom asked again but this time actually looked as if she was concerned for once.

I moved my hair out of my face and took a deep breath. "I'm fine, I'm just... tired". I lied, I didn't know how to explain what just happened, especially not to her.

"Hmm." she said as she walked away back to wherever she came from.

Callie then came and sat down on the couch next to me. We both looked at Claire as she was eating her skittles and watching cartoons not paying us any attention.

Callie took a deep breath,

"What happened back there Cait?" She asked as she put her hand on my shoulder.

"It was so weird," I paused,

"It was almost as if I had seen what was going to happen before it happened. Which is crazy right? Cause that can't happen, I mean, that's like something that can only happen in movies. Could that even be real life? I must be losing it. I must be having some type of stroke." I spoke.

Callie couldn't help but let out a giggle.

"You're not having a stroke Cait, now a mental breakdown maybe."

39

She stated. A mental breakdown? I guess that can cause me to hallucinate right?

No I'm having a stroke.

"But it felt so real."

I can tell Callie was speechless, I mean from her point of view it does sound like I'm talking crazy. I'm probably just tired and overthinking all of this.

I sighed as I looked back at Claire who was already halfway done with her skittles still all up in the cartoons she was watching. She was watching some show about a family of talking erasers, all laughing and playing together. So weird.

I sighed as I thought to myself, oh how I wish can live like those erasers right about now.

\* \* \*

Later that night, after Callie had gone home, and I had tucked Claire into bed, I couldn't help but constantly think about what happened earlier. It's like it was a movie, just replaying over and over in my head.

I decided I should probably turn in for the night, today was definitely one to remember.

I rested the back of my head against my pink fluffy pillow and stared at the ceiling. My eyes landed on a hole that had gotten there a few weeks ago. Mom and Steve had just got into a big argument when she came into my room with the broom stick and just started whacking everything. I'm not even really sure how she was able to hit up so high but, don't underestimate angry mom's ways. I continued to stare at the hole until my eyes began to get really heavy. It wasn't long before I closed them and drifted off to sleep.

* * *

"Oh gosh Callie are you seriously eating a twinkie for breakfast?" I said as I met up with Callie as we began to walk to the bus stop for school.

"Hey, don't judge me." she said as she took another huge bite out of her twinkie. The obsession that Callie has with Twinkies is insane. I laughed as shook my head and we continued to walk.

"So how did you sleep?" Callie asked in a gently tone. I actually slept like a complete baby last night, probably the best sleep I have had this week.

"Really good actually." I replied while we both stopped at the stop light as we waited for the lights to turn red so we can cross.

"Great!" Callie smiled. Callie then took her phone out of her pocket as she noticed she was getting a phone call. She answered it right as the lights turned red, we started to walk but I quickly stopped when I realized my shoelaces were untied. Callie continued to walk while still being on the phone barely paying attention to the roads.

"I'll be right there Callie!" I shouted as I bent down to tie my shoes. Just as I was finish tying them, I began to hear tires screeching and horns blowing. I looked up quickly and then right before my eyes, I seen a taxicab speeding down the street, running the red light, and aiming right for Callie.

"Callie!" I screamed, but it was too late. Before I can even process what happened I jumped up and ran as fast as I can to Callie's side. She was limped over with blood all over.

"CALLIE!" I yelled as I knelt beside her and started shaking her. She didn't budge.

"Callie wake up please!" I cried out, but still nothing. I looked around and there were people outside of their cars watching, some with cameras out, some calling 911.

"Please someone help me!" I yelled. I kept yelling and screaming until I couldn't hear anything anymore. My voice was distant once again, and there it was, my vision began to blur and my head started spinning. I couldn't see anything around me anymore, all I could hear was the strong wind.

I closed my eyes and held my breath as I waited for it to be over. The sound of the wind grew stronger and stronger within seconds. I felt the blood rush too my head as I held my breath. Soon enough it finally stopped.

I opened my eyes and looked around; I was in complete darkness. I couldn't see anything. I began to cry as my anxiety completely took over my body.

"Caitlyn." I heard a voice say,

I looked around and still couldn't see anything. I started to walk slowly with my arms stretched out in front of me trying to feel for anything.

"Caitlyn!"

I jumped up out of bed and seen my mom standing in front of me. My breathing was heavy and I held my chest as I tried to catch my breath.

"What is your problem? You're going to miss the bus get up!" She yelled at me as she walked out slamming the door behind her.

I was still having a hard time breathing. That dream felt so real. It took a few minutes but I finally calmed myself down. I got out of bed and went into the bathroom and washed my face and brushed my teeth.

I looked up at myself in the mirror and stared at the dark circles underneath my eyes. It looked like I haven't slept in months. I sighed as I dug into my makeup cabinet and applied a little bit of foundation, just enough so I don't look like a zombie anymore.

"Okay I look somewhat alive now." I said to myself. I then went back to my room to change for school. My phone started to ring as I was finishing getting ready, I looked and seen it was Callie.

"Callie oh my goodness!" I answered.

"What's wrong? Where are you? We're going to miss the bus." She replied.

"I'm coming but I need to tell you about this dream that I had last night." I said as I grabbed my shoes and put them on my feet.

"You can tell me when you get outside now hurry up." She said as she hung up the phone.

Callie was always on time and any sort of inconvenience or thought of us being late stressed her out. I finished putting on my shoes, grabbed my back pack and ran out of my room and out of the house.

I seen Callie across the street as she was jumping up and down and waving her hand motioning for me to hurry up. I looked both way before running across the street to meet up with her.

"Damn finally." She said as we began walking. I rolled my eyes playfully.

"I'm not that late." I said. "Close to it, gosh you stress me out." She said as she then reached into her back pack and pulled out a twinkie.

My mind instantly went back to my dream. But it's Callie, she's always eating a twinkie. I doubt there's any significance in this.

"Of course, you're eating a twinkie." I said and she laughed.

"Speaking of that, I dreamed that you were eating a twinkie and then-"I started but was interrupted by Callie's phone ringing.

"Oh, one second Cait, it's Mike". She said as she answered the phone and I rolled my eyes.

Ugh Mike. Callie had the biggest crush on Mike, he goes to our school and is a grade above us. Whenever he calls or texts you can forget about Callie hearing anything you say to her.

Let's just say if the roof was falling down and Callie was talking to Mike, she'd be oblivious, and the roof would be on top of her.

We continued walking to the bus stop when I then tripped over my shoe laces. They don't call me a clumsy duck for nothing.

"Dang it, keep going Callie I'll be right there." I said as I bent over to tie my shoe. Suddenly it all came back to me. My dream.

Before I even finished tying my shoe, I looked up to see Callie halfway in the street not paying attention. I then looked to my left to see the same taxi cab I see in my dream flying down.

My heart skipped a beat as I quickly got up and ran.

"Callie look!" I yelled. Callie then looked to her left and quickly ran to the side walk as the taxi kept speeding down the street missing her by an inch.

"What the fuck you asshole!" Callie yelled to the now far gone taxi cab. I sighed in relief as I looked both ways and made my way to Callie at the sidewalk.

"Oh my goodness Callie you need to pay attention to where you are going. You could have been seriously hurt!" I said to her. I started to hyperventilate again, if this ended up being anything like my dream, I would have completely lost it.

"Cait relax I'm fine." she said as she placed her hand of my back to try to calm me down. She had gotten off the phone with Mike and was now looking at me like I was crazy.

"What's wrong? Calm down I'm fine." she said again and I shook my head.

"It's just that's what I had to tell you, I dreamed of this." I finally spit out.

"I dreamed that you were eating a twinkie, got a phone call, and got hit by a car." I said and she looked bewildered.

"Are you serious?" She asked with her eyes wide open as I nodded my head.

"Yes, and in the dream, I was tying my shoe when it happened, something told me to look up before I tied it, to try to warn you". I explained.

Callie was speechless. We walked the rest of the way in complete silence until we finally reached the bus stop.

Once the bus arrived, we got on and sat in the very first seat.

"Are you okay?" I asked Callie who was just staring out the window.

"In the dream, did I die?" she asked.

"I don't know, you got hit and weren't moving or anything, I tried to wake you but then that wind that I felt when we were at the store happened and everything turned into darkness." I explained.

"That's so crazy Cait" she said and I just nodded my head.

I then see a smile creep upon her face.

"Why are you smiling?" I asked confused. This girl just almost lost her life and now she's smiling like a crazy person.

"What if you're like, psychic?" She smiled.

"You know how cool that would be? I'll have a psychic friend! You could read people's mind and mess with them. This is awesome!" she exclaimed and all I could do was laugh.

"Callie you're so weird, I am not psychic." I said as we both continued to laugh.

Psychic, the stuff that comes out of this girl's mouth. How can I be psychic? It was just a dream. I'm not psychic.

Am I?

# Chapter 7

School was over for the day and I was now back at home trying to do homework in the living room. I couldn't focus today on school at all, especially not with Callie beside me telling me all kind of scenarios that we could get into if I was really a psychic. She is such a goof.

I finally finished my homework when the knob on the front door started to turn. I sighed heavily as I knew it was mom coming in. The door opened and incomes mom and Claire.

I smiled when I see Claire walk in with her big pink backpack holding a juice box. Mom had a look of disgust on her face, so I already knew what was about to happen.

"Hey mom, hi Claire." I said as I started to gather my homework together.

"Cait!" Claire cheered as she ran to me and gave me the biggest hug. She felt a little warm as my hand touched her forehead.

"You feel hot." I said continuing to feel her face.

"Yeah she threw up all in my car, I think she's sick. You need to go to the store to pick her up some medicine." Mom said obviously disgusted.

I hated when Claire got sick, but mom hated it even more. She hates it because she's then forced to care. Although when Claire gets sick I'm usually the one who takes care of her.

"Okay, I'll go right now." I spoke.

"I go?" Claire asked looking up at me. She hated not going anywhere with me.

"Are you sure you don't want to take a nap?" I asked her and she shook her head no. I then looked at my mom who just shrugged her shoulders and walked off indicating that she didn't care if I took her or not.

"Okay come on, let's make it a quick trip though." I said and she nodded her head. Mom then came back and handed me a twenty dollar bill. I took the money, grabbed Claire's hand and we walked out.

* * *

"You want some skittles?" I asked Claire as we walked by the candy aisle.

Her eyes lit up as she smiled.

"Yes skittles" She said. I know she was sick and shouldn't eat them but I couldn't help it. She was so cute, and it's skittles, skittles makes everyone feel better.

"Grab the ones you want" I said and she walked up and grabbed a red pack of skittles. We then walked to the medicine section and I looked for a medicine that helped with fevers and stomach aches.

There was so many different kinds of medication. How on earth am I supposed to know which one to choose. I continued to pick up different ones, reading the back of it to try to figure out which one to get.

Times like this would be so much easier to have a mother to help you.

"Claire, this is hard." I said as I looked to where Claire was standing last and didn't see her.

"Claire?" I said as I did a 360 turn but she wasn't there. My heart dropped to my stomach as I took off looking for her. How did she manage to escape so quickly?

"CLAIRE?" I yelled, I seen a worker standing over by the drinks and I ran to them.

"Hi, have you see a little girl wearing a pink shirt, black pants and white shoes?" I asked describing what Claire was wearing.

"I haven't I'm sorry." the worker said. I took off again looking all over the store. I tried to keep my composure and not panic. I'm going to find her.

I then went over to the toy section and finally see Claire standing there holding hands with an old lady. I quickly ran to her and grabbed her.

"Claire you can NOT walk away from me okay?" I said breathing heavily.

"I'm sorry." She said. I then looked up at the old lady and realized it was the exact same lady who was here in the store the last time I was here.

"Um hi, thank you." I said to the older lady who was just staring at me. Her whole persona sort of creeps me out and gave me chills. I backed away slowly with Claire in my arms as we headed back to the medicine aisle.

"Claire you nearly gave me a heart attack." I said placing Claire down.

"The lady told me to come here." Claire said to me.

"Claire you cannot wonder off with strangers it's not safe." I said strictly and she nodded her head indicating she understood.

I grabbed a bottle of Pepto Bismol and headed to the front to pay. I made sure Claire stuck to me like glue. This is the second time that I have gotten such a weird vibe from that old lady. Her wrinkled face was twisted into a sinister grin, and her eyes seemed to bore into my soul. She was spine chilling.

"You come here a lot huh?" A deep voice broke me out of my thoughts. I looked up to see the store clerk, I couldn't help but stare at him. He was tall with dark hair that fell into his beautiful hazel eyes. He was a sight to see.

"Oh, um yeah I do." I giggled a bit. "I kind of live right down the street so this is like my second home." I chuckled and he smiled. Woah, his smile was so bright and infectious.

He then started to scan the two little items that we had. "So, what's your name? I feel like I've see you around school a few times." Oh gosh he goes to school with me. He must see how raggedy I look every day.

"I'm Caitlyn, this is my little sister Claire." I said pointing to Claire as she smiled at him.

"Hey Claire." He waved at her. "Hi to you too Caitlyn, I'm- "

"Carter." I said cutting him off. He looked a little confused.

"Oh, I just read your name tag." I said and he smiled. "Makes sense." he said to me as we both laughed.

"Thought you were some kind of psychic or something." he said and I laughed nervously.

"Ha psychic, that's funny." I awkwardly joked. What's up with that word?

"This is going to be $14.86." He said. I pulled out the crisp 20 dollar bill mom gave me and handed it to him. He gave me my change back and then placed my items into a small bag.

"There you go, we should hang out sometime." He said as he handed me the bag.

"Thank you." I said grabbing it. "Sure, I'd love that." I smiled. He then ripped a piece of receipt paper and started to write down his number.

I smiled as I grabbed the paper from him. "Okay see you around." he said and I waved as Claire and I walked away.

I couldn't help but smile the whole way back home.

"Why are you cheesy?" Claire asked looking up at me.

"Because a really cute boy just asked to hang out with me." I said to her and she gave me a look of disgust.

"Why that face?" I laughed. "Boys are stinky." she said holding her nose. I laughed as I held her hand and we walked back home.

This one sure didn't seem stinky.

# Chapter 8

It's been a few days since carter and I talked at the grocery store. I had never been out before with a guy, and I was nervous as I got ready. I tried on outfit after outfit, but nothing seemed right. Finally, I settled on a simple dress and some sandals.

I had to beg mom to let me go out today. I lied and told her Callie and I had plans. I just know she wouldn't ever let me go out with a guy. Claire was at a play date so I didn't have to worry about anything bad happening to her with mom.

I did a double take in the mirror and couldn't help but feel disappointed. I have always struggled with my appearance, and no matter how hard I try, I never feel beautiful enough. I look in the mirror and see every flaw, every imperfection, and it's never enough. I longed to be one of those girls who could look in the mirror and see nothing but beauty, but I just can't seem to do it. I sighed, and turned away from the mirror and I headed out.

I met Carter at the store, we had agreed on just meeting here and going to our destination, which is the park, together. I walked in and seen him sitting on one of the benches. He looked even better than I remembered. He was wearing a white t-shirt and some jeans, and he had a smile on his face that made my heart skip a beat.

"Hey," he said, walking up to me. I immediately caught a whiff of his cologne, and couldn't help but smile. It was a subtle scent, not overpowering or cloying like some colognes could be. I can't quite put my finger on what it smells like, but it was fresh and clean, with just a hint of something spicy and masculine.

"Hey," I said, feeling my face turn red. Oh come on Caitlyn don't start blushing already.

We walked around the store for a while, talking about everything and nothing. I felt so comfortable around him, like I had known him forever.

He started telling me a little about him and his family. He's 17, a year older than me. He has a little brother who is 7 and an older sister who's 20. His mom and dad divorced when he was younger and his mom remarried about 5 years ago. He then told me about his hobbies, and his dreams, and I listened intently, hanging on every word.

We grabbed a few snacks from the store and then we paid and headed out.

Suddenly, I felt a strange sensation wash over me. It was like a wave of energy that I couldn't explain, and I instantly knew what was happening.

"Are you okay?" Carter asked, looking at me with concern.

I tried to shake it off, but the feeling just kept getting stronger. Suddenly, I saw a vision. It was like a movie playing in my head, and I couldn't look away.

I saw a woman, crying in a hospital room. She was holding a baby, and I knew that it was her son. I could feel her pain, and I knew that something terrible had happened. The sensation grew stronger and soon I couldn't see the woman anymore and the vision vanished.

"Are you sure you're okay?" Carter asked again, putting his hand on my shoulder snapping me back to reality.

My hands were trembling and my knees weakened.

"Uh yeah I'm fine." I lied. "Let's just keep walking." I said and he nodded his head.

We continued walking to the park and my head began to pound a bit. I then took out my phone to text Callie.

"Callie it happened again." I messaged her. I didn't want to tell Carter anything. I don't want him looking at me all crazy and then ditching me.

After a few minutes of walking we made it to the park. The sun bathed the park in a golden hue, casting long shadows across the neatly trimmed grass. The distant laughter of children playing contrasted sharply with the urgent situation unfolding before us.

As we walked through the park, I couldn't shake the feeling that something was off. Though this has happened a few times already, this one was particularly strong.

I felt my phone vibrate in the butt of my pocket. I pulled out and seen it was Callie responding to me.

"Dude you're a psychic, what happened this time?" The message read.

"I'm sorry I'm just texting my mom can you give me a minute?" I said to Carter. I didn't want to be rude and be on my phone during our outing but I had to let Callie know.

"It wasn't like any other time with the winds or anything. This time it sort of stopped me in my tracks. My body felt stuck and it felt like a movie was being played right in front of me. There was a woman in the hospital with a baby boy. She was crying and I instantly felt her pain. I don't know what happened but I just know it was really bad. Before I can figure out what it was the vision stopped." I sent to her.

"But also out with Carter so I'll text you a little later." I double texted her as I put my phone away.

I told Callie about Carter the second I got home from the store that day. She was more excited than me.

She said it was about time someone started trying to "knock my boots off" whatever that means.

Carter and I found a little picnic table and we sat down and pulled out our snacks. I tried my best to ignore what just happened and to put it aside but the visuals were stuck in my head.

I looked at all the snacks laid out on the table and my eyes landed on a pack of skittles. I grabbed them as I thought about Claire and smiled.

"What got you all smiley?" Carter said as he looked up at me. I let out a small laugh.

"Just thinking of Claire, and her obsession with skittles." I said.

"Oh yeah I remember." He laughed. It was silent for a moment.

"I often wonder," I said, my voice tinged with a mixture of curiosity and vulnerability, "if our choices truly define who we are or if there's something deeper that shapes our paths."

Carter gazed at me intently, his eyes filled with a mixture of empathy and understanding. "I think it's a little bit of both," he replied. "Our choices are like brushstrokes on the canvas of life, but there's also an unseen force that guides us, something beyond our comprehension."

"Do you always talk like a poet?" I asked as he started to laugh. Such an infectious laugh.

"Well I have been told that I'm very articulate with my wording." He said and I smiled.

Just as I was about to respond a faint cry pierced the air interrupting our conversation.

"You hear that?" I asked as I got up from the picnic table.

"Yeah I did." Carter said standing up as well. Our heads turned simultaneously as we searched for the sound.

My heart quickened as my eyes landed on a pregnant lady lying on the ground, her face twisted in pain. Again, just like in the vision.

"Oh my God are you okay?" Carter asked as he ran to her side. For a moment I just stood there, I'm completely utter shock. But then, I quickly sprung into actions.

"Please help, my baby. Something is wrong." The lady cried.

I quickly pulled out my phone as I dialed emergency services. I explained to them the situation and where we were and they informed me they were on their way.

I knelt beside the woman. "It's going to be okay. Help is on the way. You're not alone, we're here." I said as I tried to give her comfort.

The woman, wracked with pain, looked up at me with tear-filled eyes. "Thank you." she croaked out.

As we waited for the ambulance, I kept the woman engaged in conversation, distracting her from the pain and fear. Gradually, a sense of calm settled over her, and a glimmer of hope replaced the desperation in her eyes.

Minutes later, the sound of sirens filled the air as the ambulance arrived. Paramedics rushed to the woman's side, assessing her condition and providing immediate medical care. My heart pounded with relief, as I watched the professionals take charge, confident that she would receive the help she desperately needed.

I turned to Carter, "That was really scary." I said as I let out a breath.

He smiled warmly, his eyes reflecting admiration and support. "You did amazing, there's no way I would have remained that calm."

They began to put the woman into the ambulance but before they can she stopped them. I watched as I seen her point in my direction.

One of the paramedics then nodded his hand as he started to approach me.

"The woman is asking if you can come with her to the hospital." He said. She wants me to come with her?

"Um," I hesitated as I looked at Carter.

"I'll come too." He said giving me reassurance and I smiled.

I took a deep breath, the weight of the situation sinking in. Carter's reassuring presence beside me offered a sliver of comfort midst the chaos. "Are you sure you want to come?" I asked, my voice trembling slightly.

Carter's gaze was steady, his determination clear. "I'm coming with you. You don't have to face this alone."

# Chapter 9

I stood outside the hospital room, my mind raced with a whirlwind of emotions. I looked at the woman through the small window in the door and felt the tears in my eyes start to form.

Carter stood by my side, his hand gently resting on my shoulder as we both watched the scene inside the room. The woman was put into a light coma as the doctors worked frantically to save her unborn child.

As I watched the doctors rush to perform an emergency procedure, my mind drifted back to my mom. In the moment, all of the anger and fear that I had for her suddenly vanished and I just wanted to call her.

I turned to carter and gave him a weak smile as I took my phone out of my pocket.

"Hey I'm going to call my mom really quick." I said to him. "Yeah of course." he smiled.

I walked over to the lobby and stood next to a vending machine. I dialed my mom's number and placed the phone to my ear.

Within two rings, it went straight to voicemail. I sighed as reality hit once again. It was worth a shot.

Staring into the vending machine and looking at all the snacks, I smiled as Callie came to mind. I decided to call her to update her on everything that happened.

**[Phone ringing]**

**Callie:** *[picks up]* Hey Cait! What's up?

**Caitlyn:** Callie, you won't believe what just happened. I'm still shaking.

**Callie:** Oh no, what happened? You sound serious.

**Caitlyn:** Remember the lady I told you about in my vision?

**Callie:** Oh gosh, yeah?

**Caitlyn:** Well, it actually happened. It was terrifying—I helped calm her down until the ambulance came. I think we got her here just in time.

**Callie:** Whoa, Caitlyn, this is serious stuff. Is she okay?

**Caitlyn:** I hope so. We're here at the hospital now, just waiting. They're operating on her.

**Callie:** I know this is scary, and you don't have any clue what this is or why it's happening, but I'm so proud of you, Cait. I'm serious, it's like you're a superhero or something.

**Caitlyn:** *[laughs]* Thanks, Callie. I don't feel like a superhero, though. It's just... I can't ignore these visions anymore. They're real, and they're happening for a reason. I just don't know what it is.

**Callie:** Maybe there's a purpose to all of this, Cait. Maybe you're meant to make a difference in people's lives.

**Caitlyn:** Maybe... I just wish I understood more about why this is happening to me.

**Callie:** I understand. I'm here with you and for you. We can figure it out together.

**Caitlyn:** Thanks, Callie. I appreciate all that you do.

**Callie:** Of course, Cait. That's what best friends are for. Just promise me you'll take care of yourself too, okay?

**Caitlyn:** I will. I promise.

**Callie:** So, how's Carter?

**Caitlyn:** *[blushes]* I can't even fathom...

**Callie:** YES! Knocking boots!

**Caitlyn:** *[laughs]* Bye, Callie.

**Callie:** Talk to you later, superhero!

Callie is a nut. I laughed to myself as I walked back over to Carter, who had found a bench and was sitting down on his phone.

"I'm back, sorry if I took a while." I said sitting down just a few inches away from him. He pulled me closer to him and my heart skipped a beat. Just the way his hands felt against my skin.

"No worries, although I did get pretty lonely." he said as he stared into my eyes. I looked away quick before I started to blush and turn into tinker bell. Embarrassing.

"Why do you do that?" Carter asked. I looked up at him with confusion.

"Do what?" I asked him.

"You look away and hide your face whenever I try to admire you." He stated with a serious look on his face.

"You're beautiful don't you know that?" He asked and I just froze. Why is this boy digging into my soul right now?

"If you don't know, then I'm going to tell you. If there is one thing that you should believe me or trust me on, it's this. I've never seen anyone as beautiful as you. Your inner beauty overrides the world, and your outer beauty matches all that's within. So when I want to admire that, I need you to own it. I don't know what you have been through or what you have heard about yourself but it's time you start gaining your power back." He finished and my eyes were glossy.

No one has ever said that to me before. It's something about Carter I can't put my finger on it. He's just so gentle. I've never had gentle.

"Okay I will." I said softly looking him deep into his eyes without looking away. We stared at each other as he held my hand rubbing the top of it gently with his thumb, until we looked away and sat comfortably in silence.

As the minutes stretched into hours, still inside of the hospital waiting room, a doctor emerged from the room, a tired but hopeful expression on his face. He explained that the woman and her baby had both made it through the surgery and everything went smoothly.

I couldn't help but feel a sense of relief wash over me.

"Thank you so much, can I go see her?" I asked.

"Yes you may go see her." He said as he pointed to the room in which the woman was it. I thanked him again by giving him a nod and a warm smile. I looked at carter wondering if he was going to come with me or not.

"You go," he said.

"I'll be right out here waiting for you." he added. I turned to go inside of the room. I walked in and the woman was laying there in bed holding a beautiful baby.

Her eyes lit up and her smile grew wider when she seen me enter the room.

I approached her bed slowly, still overwhelmed by the intensity of the last few hours. Her eyes, tired yet filled with gratitude, met mine as I stood beside her. The newborn in her arms stirred, and I couldn't help but smile at the sight of new life.

"You're an angel," she whispered hoarsely.

"Thank you for everything you did."

Tears welled up in my eyes. "I'm just glad everything turned out okay." I managed to say, my voice barely above a whisper.

She nodded, her gaze shifting to the tiny bundle in her arms.

"Do you have a name?" I asked staring at the baby.

"I'm going to name him after his father, Christian." She smiled with tears in her eyes.

"That's beautiful, where is he? I bet he can't wait to meet him." I smiled but her smile turned into a frown.

I instantly knew what she was going to say.

"He actually died about a week ago." She said as my heart shattered.

"I am so sorry." I empathized. That must be incredibly tough," I replied softly, my heart aching for her loss. "But I'm sure he's watching over both of you now, proud that his son made it through with such a strong mother."

She nodded, tears now flowing freely. "Thank you," she managed to say midst her emotions. "Thank you for saving us."

I reached out and gently squeezed her hand, offering whatever comfort I could in that moment. "You're so strong," I murmured, feeling a lump in my throat.

"Christian will always be a part of your son's life, in spirit." She smiled faintly through her tears, a gesture of resilience that touched me deeply. "I believe that too," she whispered, her voice filled with conviction.

I stayed with her for a while longer, offering words of encouragement and support. I looked at the time and realized I had to go soon.

"I have to go but I'm so glad you're okay. Also I never did get your name." I chuckled.

She chuckled back, "Kiya" she smiled.

"Well it was nice meeting you Kiya, you too baby Christian." I smiled. Kiya waved as she blew me a kiss goodbye.

I stepped out the door to find Carter waiting just outside the door.

He looked up as I approached, concerned look on his face. "How is she?" he asked quietly.

"She's strong," I replied, my voice still tinged with emotion. "And the baby, Christian, he's a fighter."

Carter nodded, his hand finding mine once again.

"You did a remarkable thing today," he said softly, his eyes reflecting admiration. "I'm so proud of you."

Butterflies flew around in my stomach again as I leaned into him, grateful for his presence. "Thank you for being here," I whispered, feeling a sense of peace settle over me.

Together, we walked out of the hospital, still amazed by everything that happened today. I think this may be my calling. I'm not sure, but there has to be a reason as to why this is happening to me. I think it's about time I look more into it.

# Chapter 10

The morning sun filtered through the classroom windows as Callie and I settled into our usual seats at the back of the classroom. My mind was still reeling from yesterday's events at the hospital. Callie must have sensed my distraction because she leaned over and whispered, "You okay, Cait?"

I nodded, though my thoughts were far from okay. "I just can't stop thinking about the visions and everything."

Callie gave me a sympathetic look. "Maybe there's something we can do to figure it out. Have you thought about talking to someone who might know more about this kind of thing?"

"I don't even know where to start," I admitted, frustration lacing my words. "I mean, it's not like there's a 'Visions 101' class I can take."

Callie smiled. "Where's Carter?" she asked, trying to distract me. I smiled as I thought about him.

"He's actually not here today, his mom is taking him and his family on a cruise for the weekend." I said.

Our teacher, Ms. Smith entered the room, and the chatter died down. As the lesson began, I found it hard to focus. My mind kept drifting back to Kiya and baby Christian. Everything just seemed unreal.

During lunch, Callie and I sat outside under our favorite tree and started to talk.

"You know what I have been thinking about?" I said to Callie who was on her phone. She looked up at me, "what?" she asked.

"The vision that I had of Kiya showed her in the hospital room holding a baby but she was distraught, almost like the baby might have been hurt or you know.. not alive." I explained.

"But they were both okay.. so was my vision wrong?" I asked. I was so confused. Kiya met the perfect description of my vision in real life, but she was okay in the end.

"I think that your vision this time was maybe a warning, you know? Maybe if you weren't there and if you didn't get to her in time, the vision that you seen would have actually happened. Meaning she might have lost her baby if you didn't help her." Callie stated.

"Think about it, you had a vision of me getting hit by a car right?" Callie asked and I nodded my head. "But you pushed me out of the way in time. Imagine if I had walked by myself and you weren't there." she said. I couldn't believe any of this. It was truly like a movie.

"Then there was the truck," Callie uttered.

"But I couldn't stop the truck." I admitted.

"No but you didn't know what was happening at the time. That was your very first vision." She said as she pulled out a sandwich she had in her lunch box.

"You're right." I replied. I thought about all the visions that I have seen so far and sighed. It just seemed to weird to be true.

"Maybe there's a book in the library about this kind of stuff," Callie suggested between bites of her sandwich.

"Maybe," I agreed. "I'll check after school."

We were halfway through our conversation when I saw Josh, the school jerk, striding across the courtyard. He sneered at a group of younger kids, making them scatter like frightened birds. I felt a familiar tug in my mind, and before I knew it, another vision overtook me.

I saw Josh in a small, dimly lit living room. A man, presumably his father, loomed over him, shouting angrily, waving a bottle of beer up and down. Josh cowered, his face a mix of fear and defiance. The man raised his hand, and I flinched as he struck Josh across the face. I thought the hit would have been it, but his father just kept on going. Hitting him non stop as Josh cried. The vision faded, leaving me shaken.

"Cait, what's wrong?" Callie asked, noticing my sudden pallor and snapping me back into reality.

I took a deep breath, trying to steady myself. "I just had another one. It was about Josh."

Callie's eyes widened. "Ew. Josh? What did you see?"

"His father...he's abusing him," I whispered, the words heavy on my tongue. I know all about abuse.

Callie's expression softened with understanding. "That explains a lot. No wonder he's always so angry and mean."

I nodded, my heart aching for Josh. "I never would have guessed."

"We should tell someone," Callie said firmly. "A teacher or a counselor. They can help." She added.

"I-I don't know." I stuttered.

"What do you mean?" Callie said confused. For starters, I don't even know if the vision I just had was even real I mean come on, I don't even know what this even is yet. What if its just my head? What if he isn't actually being abused and I'm just like overthinking or something?

"I don't know Callie I think we should wait a little." I said and she gave me a look of concern. "Cait, this was another vision, we cant just sit and let it keep happening." She said as she finally put her sandwich down.

"What if it wasn't a vision though?" I asked looking down. I just couldn't come to terms with this happening.

"Cait, I know it may seem super crazy and unbelievable right now but your visions are real. How else would you explain everything else you've seen?" She voiced.

"I don't know.. a coincidence?" I said unsure. Callie sighed heavily in frustration. It's easy for her to just want to up and reveal everything, it's not happening to her. The thought of revealing my vision to an adult or anyone was daunting. How could I explain without sounding crazy?

"Oh Cait." Callie said. "Okay even if I do go and tell someone, what if Josh doesn't want anyone to know, I mean.. its kind of like what I'm going through." I said my thoughts being taken back to my own life. My predicament is pretty bad, but at the same time, Id rather stay where I am than have my mom locked up and Claire and I taken away and separated into some lousy foster care system.

"Okay Cait, I guess you're right. The ball is in your court, whatever you want to do." Callie said giving a soft smile. She softens up every time I mention anything about my life at home.

I nodded my head and sighed as I lied back onto the tree. If Josh really is being abused, that would be heart breaking. I actually really hope this vision wasn't true.

After school, Callie and I went to the library. While Callie looked through the shelves for books on psychic phenomena, I walked over to the computers.

I searched up different stories on psychic experiences and people who have visions. So many articles popped up, different people with different stories. Every single one got deeper and more crazy as the list went on.

As I scrolled through the search results, my eyes were drawn to a headline that struck me as oddly familiar: *"Local Woman Claims to See Spirits - Psychic Predictions and Mysterious Appearances."* The article was accompanied by a grainy photo of a woman with striking features.

I gasped as I realized that this is the same woman I had seen in the store. Her gaze was unnervingly penetrating. I clicked on the article, my heart pounding. It was about a woman named Elanor Fox, who had gained local notoriety for her supposed psychic abilities. The article described how Elanor had made numerous predictions about events that had later come true. Eyewitnesses claimed that Elanor had an eerie, otherworldly presence and was often seen in various locations, seemingly drawn to people who were in distress or danger.

The more I read, the more unsettling it became. The article detailed Elanor's background, noting her reputation for giving cryptic warnings and her almost spectral presence. Witnesses described her as someone who seemed to drift through life, her gaze often fixed on people as if she was peering into their very souls. I remembered those exact unsettling encounters with the woman. Elanor had never spoken a word, only stared at me with those penetrating eyes.

But then my eyes froze on the final lines of the article:

*"Despite her mysterious presence, it was revealed in a recent investigation that Elanor Fox passed away three years ago. The cause of death was reported as a sudden illness. Her haunting appearances have since puzzled many, as some believe her spirit may still be wandering, or that there is another explanation entirely."*

My breath hitched. Elanor fox has been dead for years, yet I seen her not once, but twice. The article's final statement only deepened the mystery: *"Is Elanor Fox a lingering spirit, or is there something else at play?"*

A cold shiver ran down my spine. The idea that I was seeing someone who had been dead for years was both terrifying and confusing. My fingers trembled as I closed the article, my mind racing with questions. Why was I seeing her? Was it connected to my own visions? Is this some type of sinister shit? Am I fucking haunted?

"Callie," I called out, my voice shaky. "I need to show you something."

Callie looked up from a book she had been skimming through, noticing my distress. She walked over quickly, her eyes filled with concern. "What's wrong?"

"Remember the old woman I told you about in the store?" I asked hoping she would remember.

"Um," she said trying to think back.

Callie was to indulged into her twinkie to remember.

"Ugh Callie when you were eating your twinkie and I told you that the weird message popped up on the TV screen." I said and her eyes lit up.

"Oh! Yes! That twinkie was so fresh." she said and I rolled my eyes.

I turned the computer screen towards her, showing her the article about the woman.

"This is the lady. I seen her another time right after when I went to the store with Claire." I said tapping the computer screen with my finger expeditiously.

Callie's eyes widened as she read the headline and then the final lines about Elanor's death.

"Well this... this doesn't make sense," Callie said, her voice low. "You've seen her in the store, and now she's been dead for years?"

"Are you sure it's her?" She added

"Yes! I remember the features. Her winkles and creepy smile. Its her!" I shouted.

"Shhh." A random girl whispered in the library.

"Oh fuck off." Callie said sticking her middle finger at her.

"Oh my gosh Callie stop." I said embarrassed. "I'm sorry." I mouthed to the girl who just rolled her eyes in return.

"I don't know what's happening," I said, my voice trembling. "But there has to be a reason why I keep seeing her. What if my visions and her appearances are somehow connected?"

Callie looked at me, her expression thoughtful.

"I'm stressed out. I'm having these weird visions, I'm seeing ghosts and shit, what the hell is happening." I said on the verge of pulling my hair out.

"Okay lets take a deep breath" Callie said. She started to deep breathe and I followed. We continued that for another 30 seconds until I calmed down a bit.

"Okay, now look at what I found." Callie said holding up a book titled "The Unseen World: Understanding Psychic Phenomena."

"Seems interesting, you should read it." She said. I grabbed the book, it was thick and had a bunch of pages missing from it. Looked old as if it was something that was made back in the 1900's.

"Looks dirty." I said and she laughed. "Just get it, might be something informative in there." I just gave in and went to check out the book.

We gathered our belongings and then headed out of the library. We had to walk home today because we missed the bus from going to the library.

The setting sun cast long shadows across the sidewalk. I clutched the old book tightly, the weight of its worn pages a stark contrast to the swirling chaos in my mind. The evening air was cool, but I felt a growing heat of anxiety and curiosity.

Callie and I walked in silence for a while, both lost in our own thoughts. The streets were busier now, people heading home from work or running last-minute errands. I kept glancing at the book in my hands, its title a reminder of the mysteries I was trying to unravel.

When we finally reached my house, I turned to Callie. "Thanks for helping me with this. I really appreciate it."

She gave me a reassuring smile. "No problem, Cait. We're in this together. We'll figure it out."

I nodded, feeling a bit more grounded with her support. "Yeah, we will."

# Chapter 11

I sat at home in the living room, the old book Callie had given me resting in my lap. The evening light streamed through the window, casting warm patterns on the pages. My thoughts drifted back to the hospital and Kiya. Along with the vision I had of Josh. I was still processing everything, trying to understand the strangeness of it all. I flipped through the book, its cover worn and edges frayed. It felt like a relic from another time, but I was hoping it might hold some answers.

I was deeply engrossed in the book when my phone rang, jolting me out of my concentration. I glanced at the screen, my heart skipping a beat when I saw Carter's name. I wasn't expecting him to call from his cruise, and I quickly answered.

"Hey, Carter!" I said, trying to keep my voice steady.

"Hey, Caitlyn," he replied, his voice warm and reassuring. "I didn't know if I'd be able to reach you. How are you holding up?"

I couldn't help but smile at the sound of his voice. "I'm okay. Just at home, reading this book Callie gave me. How's the cruise?"

"It's great, but I'm missing you. I wanted to check in and see how you're doing after everything that happened," he said.

"I'm really glad you called," I told him, my voice softening. "It's been a lot to process, but talking to you helps." I blushed.

We talked for a while, catching up on just the one little day we missed with each other. It was comforting to hear about his cruise adventures, even if it was just a small distraction from the whirlwind of emotions I was dealing with. As we wrapped up our conversation, I felt a bit more at ease.

After we hung up, I went back to reading the book, hoping it would provide some insight. Just as I was getting back into it, I heard the front door open. Steve, my mom's boyfriend, had come home early. I tensed, knowing that our interactions were always appalling.

"Hey, Caitlyn," Steve said as he walked into the room.

"Hi." I replied, keeping my tone neutral.

I tried to focus on the book, but Steve's presence was distracting. He plopped down on the couch and started chatting about his day. I barely registered his words as my mind remained on the book. I could feel frustration building inside me.

"Why don't you ever seem interested in what's going on in the house?" Steve said suddenly, breaking the silence.

I looked up, my patience wearing thin. "I'm just trying to read, Steve. I don't see why you're making a big deal out of it."

Steve snorted. "You know, you'd be better off doing something more productive. Like actually engaging with the people around you."

I could feel my patience fraying. "I'm not in the mood for your games, Steve."

He leaned forward, smirking as he stood up and moved toward the couch. His breath was uncomfortably close to my neck as he leaned over. "Maybe you need a little distraction," he said, his hand reaching out and brushing against my arm in a way that made my skin crawl.

I recoiled, my heart racing. "Steve, move—"

Just then, the front door swung open, and my mom walked in with Claire, her somewhat smiley demeanor fading as she saw what was happening.

"What's going on here?" she asked, her tone immediately shifting from casual to mad as she took in Steve's looming figure and my distressed face.

"Mom, Steve was just—" I started to explain, but Steve cut me off.

"Nothing's going on," Steve said quickly, his voice suddenly too smooth. "Just having a bit of fun. Caitlyn's being overly sensitive, you know how she is."

"This asshole was about to kiss me and touch me." I yelled my voice trembling with a mixture of anger and desperation.

My mom's face hardened as she glared at me. "Don't you dare lie to me Caitlyn, I know you've got a knack for causing drama."

"But mom I'm telling the truth." I pleaded my heart racing. "He was-"

"I said enough!" Mom snapped cutting me off. "Steve has been nothing but good to us, he's been patient with your mood swings and your constant complaining. You got no right to make up stories about him." She yelled at me.

I felt a sinking feeling in my chest as I stared at my mom shocked by her harsh words. "I'm not lying, why don't you ever believe anything that I say to you." My eyes glistened.

"Oh save the dramatic bullshit." She said, her voice icy and unyielding. "You think you can just make wild accusations and get away with it? You are nothing but a liar, always stirring up trouble and trying to make everyone's life miserable." Her words cut deep, each insult feeling like a fresh wound. I can't believe she thinks i would make something like this up.

I looked over at Claire who was staring at all of us with a gloomy look on her face.

"Claire can you go upstairs?" I asked her nicely yet still stressed out. She listened and went upstairs quickly.

"I'm not making any accusations, I'm telling you what happened." I said my attention back on my mom.

"Maybe if you weren't so damn insistent on playing the victim all the time we wouldn't have these problems." She spat. The sting of her accusations left me reeling.

"I'm not—"

"Shut up!" Mom shouted. "I'm sick of your lies and your attitude. You are a spoiled little liar who's always causing problems. I'm done with you and your games." I felt a wave of despair and rage as I struggled to comprehend how she can really turn against me completely.

Without another word I grabbed my book and stormed out of the house, slamming the door behind me with all the force I could muster. The sound echoed in the stillness of the streets as I fled. The cool evening air hit my face but it did little to cool the anger boiling inside me. I walked aimlessly tears streaming down my face.

That's when I saw her—the old woman from the store. My heart raced.

The woman was standing at the end of the block, her gaze fixed on me. I felt a shiver run down my spine, but this time, I was determined to confront her.

"Hey!" I called out as I approached her.

She didn't respond, just continued walking. I quickened my pace to catch up with her. The woman led me to a small, secluded park that I had never noticed before.

Oh she's about to kill me.

"Why do you keep showing up?" I demanded. "What do you want from me?"

The woman remained silent, her eyes locked on mine. As we stood there, I felt a strange sensation wash over me, like I was being pulled into a dream. Colors and images swirled around me, and I was suddenly in a vision.

I saw a scene unfold before me: a young girl in a room, struggling to understand her surroundings. Her life was filled with confusion and fear.

The vision faded as quickly as it had appeared, leaving me standing in the park, breathless and disoriented. The old woman remained still, her gaze unyielding, but something in her expression softened. It was almost as if she understood the turmoil I was going through.

I tried to steady my breath, my mind racing to piece together the fragments of the vision. The young girl—was that supposed to be me? Was this some sort of message or warning? I could feel the weight of the book in my hand, its pages seeming to hum with a new intensity.

"Please," I said, my voice trembling. "I need to understand what's happening. Why am I seeing these things?"

The woman took a slow, deliberate step toward me. Her eyes, though aged, seemed to hold a deep, knowing light. She reached into her coat pocket and pulled out a small, intricately carved wooden box. Holding it out to me, she said, "This is for you."

I hesitated, eyeing the box with suspicion and curiosity. "What's inside?" Well I guess I can just open it.

The woman didn't answer, but her eyes conveyed a sense of urgency and significance. I took the box from her hands, its surface cool and smooth against my fingers. As I opened it, I found a delicate locket nestled inside, its gold chain shimmering in the dim light.

"Why are you giving me this?" I asked, still trying to piece together the connection between the locket and the vision I'd experienced.

The old woman's lips curved into a faint, enigmatic smile. "Sometimes, finding the answers requires a journey of its own. This locket holds a clue. Trust in yourself, Caitlyn. The path will reveal itself when you are ready."

How does she know my name? What the hell is this?

Before I could respond, the woman turned and began walking away, her steps as silent as a whisper. I watched her disappear into the night, my mind buzzing with questions.

The vision and the mysterious woman had left me with more questions than answers, but I could sense that this was a step toward understanding the larger picture.

I walked back home, the night air now feeling more like a companion than a threat. The locket felt warm in my palm.

When I arrived back at the house, the confrontation with my mom and Steve still echoed in my mind. I took a deep breath and walked inside, bracing myself for the tension that awaited me. But as I approached the living room, I noticed my mom and Steve were no longer there. They must have gone into their room. Claire, who had come downstairs, looked up at me with a sympathetic expression.

"Cait okay?" she asked quietly.

I nodded, though my heart was still heavy. "I'm okay." I smiled.

Claire gave me a small grin. "Hug?" She said reaching out her arms.

I walked over to her and embraced her for a brief moment, the weight of the day's chaos and the sting of my mother's harsh words seemed to dissipate.

I gently pulled back and looked into Claire's innocent eyes, seeing the trust and love that only a child can give. "Thank you, Claire," I said softly, brushing a stray lock of hair from her face.

She simply nodded, her gaze full of understanding beyond her years. "Read with me?" she asked, holding up her favorite storybook.

I couldn't help but smile. The idea of sitting with Claire and losing ourselves in a story seemed like the perfect antidote to the turmoil I was feeling. "Sure," I agreed.

We settled into the couch, Claire snuggling beside me as I opened the book. The pages, filled with colorful illustrations and comforting words I felt a sense of peace wash over me.

As I read aloud, Claire's eyes grew heavy with sleep. Her breathing slowed, and I could feel her tiny body relaxing against mine. I continued to read softly, my voice a steady anchor in the sea of my thoughts.

The events of the day—the confrontation with Steve, the cryptic message from the old woman—seemed distant now. In this quiet, shared moment, I found solace.

When the book was finished, Claire was fast asleep, her head resting on my shoulder. I carefully closed the book and placed it on the coffee table, taking a moment to savor the calm. I looked down at the locket still clutched in my hand, its significance still unclear but somehow less daunting now.

I would face the challenges of tomorrow when the sun rose. For tonight, I had found a small haven in my sister's presence, and that was enough.

I gently adjusted Claire's blanket and stood up, carrying her to her room. As I tucked her in and kissed her forehead, I headed out and into my own room.

I guess mom and Steve finally called it a night, the house was oddly quiet. I didn't care to think about it any longer for the night. With a deep breath, I made my way to my room, exhausted.

I held the locket in my hand, and stared up at the ceiling. Thinking of all the events that has happened this week, I then drifted off into a deep sleep.

# Chapter 12

The morning light filtered softly through the curtains, but my head felt like it was being pounded by a drum. I woke up with a headache that I couldn't seem to shake, the throbbing persistent and insistent. I groaned, pressing my fingers to my temples, trying to find some relief. The images of the vision from the old woman seemed to swirl around in my mind, intensifying the pain.

After a few minutes of struggling to clear my head, I decided to get out of bed. The cool air of the room was a welcome distraction from the heat of the headache. I took a deep breath, focusing on the sound of my own breathing as I tried to steady myself. I thought about the vision, the young girl, the confusion, the sense of searching for answers.

Despite my discomfort, I knew I needed to get Claire out for some fresh air. I texted Callie, asking if she'd join us at the park. If there was one thing that usually helped clear my mind, it was spending time outside, especially with my best friend and sister.

I got dressed and then went and got Claire dressed. I fixed her some cereal to eat for breakfast and then we headed out and met Callie at her house."Claire!" Callie exclaimed as she seen Claire. Claire ran to her and jumped into her arms.

"Hey, Caitlyn!" Callie greeted me with a smile. "You look a little pale. Are you okay?"

"I'm just dealing with a headache," I said, forcing a smile. "I'm hoping some fresh air will help."

Callie gave me a sympathetic look. "Rough night last night?" She asked and I nodded my head. "You have no idea, I'll explain once we get to the park." I glanced at Claire to indicate I didn't want her to overhear the details.

When we arrived at the park, the sun was bright, and the air was filled with the sounds of children playing. Claire's face lit up as she saw the playground, and she dashed off to join in the fun.

I pulled out a blanket and sat it on the grass, Callie had bought a bag of snack cakes and chips and other picnic type things. I took a deep breath and sat on top of the blanket. I grabbed a can of soda that Callie had bought. I felt a pain of hesitation knowing I had to tell Callie what all happened.

I took a deep breath trying to steady my voice. "Callie there's something else I need to tell you" I began, my fingers nervously tracing the rim of my soda can.

"It's about Steve."

Callie's eyebrows furrowed in concern. "What about Steve?"

I hesitated, the memory of the confrontation with Steve still fresh and painful.

"Last night after you gave me the book, I came home and.." I paused struggling to find the right words.

"Steve.. he tried to.. well, he tried to kiss me and touch me, it was really uncomfortable and I felt like he was trying to cross a line."

Again.

Callie's eyes widened her expression shifting from concern to shock. "Oh my God Caitlyn that's horrible"

"He didn't go all the way." I interrupted my voice trembling

"But it was clear that he was trying to, I told my mom but she didn't believe me, she actually yelled at me and said I was lying" Callie's face twisted with anger and sympathy.

"That's awful, I'm so sorry you had to go through that. Your mom should have believed you."

"I thought she would." I said tears welling up in my eyes.

"But she just took Steve's side. I felt like she was completely against me, like she's always been." I sighed.

Callie reached out and took my hand squeezing it gently.

"You're not alone in this, I believe you and I'm here for you we'll figure this out together."

I nodded feeling a small sense of relief.

"Thanks Callie, I really needed to hear that" I smiled.

"We should report this." Callie suggested, her tone resolute.

Here she goes always trying to report things.

"Not just to clear your name but to make sure Steve doesn't do this to anyone else, it's important." She explained.

I bit my lip considering her words. "I don't know if it'll change anything especially with my mom backing him up, but maybe you're right I'll think about it." Callie nodded, her eyes full of determination.

"And don't worry about your mom, sometimes people need time to see things clearly. Right now you need to focus on protecting yourself and Claire." She stated firmly.

I nodded in agreement.

"Then after that," I started. "There's more?" She asked nervously.

"Yes, but not about Steve. After that I stormed out and ran into the old woman again." I said and her eyes widened.

"What happened?" Called asked curiously.

"She literally led me to a park." I started,

"A park? Are you nuts? Do you have a death wish or something?" She asked.

"Just listen," I said. "At the park she showed me like, this vision." I rubbed my temples, trying to ease the throbbing pain. "It was a scene with a young girl she was scared and looking basically confused as shit.

Like I can't put it into words but she looked hopeless and like she was searching for something." I continued.

"Anyways, after the vision, the woman gave me this." I said taking out the gold locket from my pocket.

Callie took it from my hands and inspected it.

"This is ugly as shit." She said and I laughed.

"She gave it to me and said 'sometimes, finding the answers requires a journey of its own'."

"Huh?" Callie asked and I laughed again.

"I don't know it was weird."

"Well, usually I would say throw it away before you become possessed or something but I don't know I guess you should just hold on to it." Callie spoke.

I looked up to check on Claire to make sure she was still in sight. I seen her playing with a group of toddlers.

As Callie and I talked, I couldn't shake the feeling that something was going to happen. That's when I spotted him, Josh. I felt a jolt of recognition. Callie noticed my sudden change in demeanor.

"Are you okay?" she asked, glancing in the direction I was staring.

"Yeah, it's just... Josh is here," I said quietly.

Callie looked up at him and tooted her nose.

"Are you thinking about talking to him?" Callie asked, her voice filled with curiosity and concern.

I hesitated, nervously fidgeting with the edge of the blanket. "I'm not sure. He's not exactly the warmest dude."

Callie gave me a reassuring look. "It's up to you, but if you're thinking of the vision you saw, then it might be worth a shot."

I took a deep breath and glanced over at Josh, still standing alone with an unreadable expression. "Alright, I'll go talk to him." I decided, standing up and brushing off my clothes.

As I approached him, I could feel my heart pounding. His eyes narrowed when he saw me, and he sneered. "Woah! The whore decided to get out of the house I see. Oh and is that a new outfit? Wow miracles do happen." He smirked.

I ignored his jibe and focused on the bruise on his cheek. "What happened there?" I asked pointing to the dark purple spot on his face.

He tried to play it cool, his voice rough. "Got into a fight with some kid. It's nothing."

I wasn't convinced. "Josh, you don't have to pretend. If you're in trouble or need help, it's okay to talk about it."

Josh's face hardened, his anger palpable. "What are you talking about? I don't need help. I'm never in trouble and it's none of your business anyway."

"It is if you're hurt," I replied, keeping my voice steady and compassionate.

His face flushed with anger and embarrassment. "I said it's nothing. Just drop it, alright?"

Seeing he wasn't going to open up, I took a step back. "Alright."

Josh turned abruptly and walked away, his steps brisk and angry. I watched him go, feeling a mix of frustration and concern. I headed back to Callie, who was waiting with a worried look.

"So, what happened?" Callie asked as I sat down.

"He was really defensive and said he got into a fight. He didn't want to talk about it," I explained. "I tried". I said giving up.

Callie nodded, acknowledging my effort. "You did and that's all that matters." She said.

Just then, a loud, harsh voice cut through the park's background noise. Callie and I turned to see Josh's father storming into the playground, his face red with fury.

"Josh! What did I tell you about leaving without letting me know." His voice was filled with rage as he approached Josh, who was visibly shrinking away.

"That's his dad." I said to Callie.

The situation escalated quickly. Josh's father grabbed him roughly and began shouting at him, his anger turning physical as he started hitting Josh.

My heart sank as I processed the horrific scene. I grabbed Callie's arm, my voice trembling. "What do we do? We have to do something"

Callie nodded, her face pale with shock. "We need to get help. Now."

My heart pounded as I watched the scene unfold. I turned to Callie, urgency in my voice. "Callie, go get Claire and take her back to the picnic area and stay there. I'm going to call for help."

Callie nodded and quickly went to guide Claire away from the commotion. I watched them go, then turned my attention back to the confrontation. I took a deep breath and pulled out my phone, dialing the number for parks security.

"Hello, my name is Caitlyn," I said when someone answered. "There's an emergency at the playground. There's a man hitting a boy. We need help immediately."

The security officer's response was quick and reassuring. "We're sending a team right away. Stay where you are and keep yourself safe."

I hung up and moved closer to the scene, trying to stay out of sight while keeping an eye on what was happening. Within minutes, I saw the security team arrive, their presence causing Josh's father to pause momentarily.

The officers intervened, speaking sternly to Josh's father. The situation was tense, but their authority was effective. They managed to subdue him and put him into custody, taking him away from the playground. I felt a mix of relief and sadness as I watched Josh's father being led away, his anger still evident but his grip on Josh finally broken.

Josh, who had been cowering against a swing set, looked up with a mix of rage and confusion. His eyes locked on me, and he stormed over, his face flushed with anger.

"Why did you have to get involved?!" Josh shouted, his voice trembling with fury. "You just made everything worse! Now my dad's going to be even more pissed!"

I took a step back, trying to keep my voice calm despite the rising tension. "Josh, I'm sorry. I couldn't watch you get beat on like that. It's not right."

His anger was palpable once again, and he shook his head. "You don't get it. You don't know what it's like. You think you can just fix everything by calling for help? You don't know what's going to happen now."

I felt a pang of guilt and helplessness but stood my ground. "I do understand. I wasn't trying to fix everything, I just wanted him to stop hurting you."

Josh glared at me, his frustration evident. "Just stay out of it. You don't understand anything. You've only made things worse."

Josh turned away, his shoulders hunched as he walked toward a quieter part of the playground. I watched him go, feeling frustrated. I knew something like this would happen which is why I didn't want to say anything to anyone when I first had the vision.

I walked back to Callie and Claire, who were waiting anxiously by the picnic area. Callie's face showing concern. "What happened? Is everything okay?"

I took a deep breath, my voice tired. "The police took Josh's dad into custody" I said.

"Well that's good right?" She asked.

"Josh is pissed. He said I just made things worse. I knew this would happen." I said irritated.

Callie gave me a comforting look. "You did the right thing, Caitlyn. Sometimes people lash out when they're hurt and scared. He might not see it now, but you helped him."

I nodded, even though deep down I know that I helped him in this moment but not overall.

Claire tugged at my hand, looking up with wide eyes. "Is dirty boy okay?" Claire asked and I hid a smirk.

She's known Josh as dirty boy for a while now because that's what Callle and I use to call him.

I smiled at her. "He will be."

As we finished packing up and headed towards the park's exit, I started to feel the throbbing in my temples yet again. The headache that had been lurking all day was now pounding mercilessly, and my vision seemed to blur. I struggled to keep my balance, clutching the picnic basket as I walked. The stress of the morning was clearly taking a toll on me.

"Caitlyn, are you okay?" Callie's voice came through, laced with concern.

I tried to nod, but the pain made me sway. "I'm fine. Just feeling a bit dizzy."

Before I could say more, the world tilted, and my legs gave out beneath me. I collapsed onto the grass, the throbbing in my head intensifying. I heard Callie's panicked voice call out for help.

"Someone, please! My friend needs help!" Callie's voice was urgent as she waved her arms, drawing attention from nearby park-goers.

I felt hands on my shoulders, but everything seemed distant and muffled. When I finally opened my eyes, I saw Callie and a couple of strangers hovering over me. My vision was still fuzzy, and I tried to focus on their faces.

"Caitlyn, are you okay?" Callie's face was full of worry.

I took a deep breath, forcing a weak smile. "I'm okay. I was just dizzy. I've been dealing with a headache all day."

The paramedics arrived quickly, checking me over as I lay on the ground. They asked me a series of questions, and I answered them as best as I could. Despite their reassurances, I was still overwhelmed by the pounding in my head.

As I lay there, trying to steady my breathing, my vision suddenly shifted again. This time, I was no longer at the park but on a luxurious cruise ship. The scene was vibrant, with sunlight glinting off the water and guests milling around the deck.

And there was Carter. He stood by the railing, looking out at the ocean with a thoughtful expression. He was dressed in casual cruise attire, but something about his posture seemed off—he was tense and distracted, not enjoying the picturesque view as one would expect. He was holding a letter in his hand, his fingers gripping it tightly. The letter had a red wax seal, and the corners were worn, as if it had been handled many times.

I struggled to make sense of the vision, but it faded as quickly as it had appeared. The deck, the letter, Carter they all slipped away, leaving me with a lingering sense of unease.

"Caitlyn?" Callie's voice brought me back to reality. "Are you sure you're okay?"

I blinked, focusing on her concerned face. "Yeah, I'm fine."

The paramedics helped me to my feet, and Callie's supportive arm wrapped around me. "Let's get you home," she said softly, her worry evident. "You need to rest."

I nodded. The vision of Carter replayed in my head. Whatever the letter said obviously worried him. As we walked away from the park, I tried to push the vision to the back of my mind, focusing instead on getting through the rest of the day.

Back at home, the comfort of familiar surroundings did little to ease my racing mind. Callie helped me settle onto the couch, her presence a steady reassurance.

"Just rest," she said softly, handing me a glass of water. "We'll figure everything out. One step at a time."

I nodded, grateful for her support. Closing my eyes, I let the fatigue wash over me, hoping that a bit of rest would bring some clarity. But even as I drifted off, the images of Josh's bruises, the old woman's locket, and Carter's worried face continued to swirl in my thoughts, a tangled web of questions that demanded answers.

Later, I told myself. Later, I will figure it out. Right now, I need a nap.

# Chapter 13

The morning bell rang, signaling the start of another week. The hallways buzzed with the usual Monday morning chatter, but I was only half listening. My headache from the weekend had dulled, but the visions still haunted me, particularly the one of Carter on the cruise ship with that letter.

I spotted Carter by his locker, looking fine as hell, as always. As much as I tried to play it off, my heart still skipped a beat whenever I saw him. Today, though, it wasn't just about my feelings, it was about finding out what that letter was.

"Hey, Carter," I greeted him, trying to sound casual.

He looked up, flashing his signature grin. "Hey, Caitlyn." He smiled, reaching in for a hug.

I wrapped him into a hug, the smell of his cologne hitting my nostrils. Oh he just smells so good.

Letting go of the hug, I leaned against the locker beside his. "I was thinking about skipping first period. You down?" I asked.

Carter raised an eyebrow, intrigued. "Skipping class? Who are you and what have you done with Caitlyn?"

I laughed, a little too brightly. "I just need a break from Ms. Smith's monotone voice. Besides, I haven't had a chance to hear about your cruise."

Carter's expression softened, and he closed his locker with a click.

"Alright, let's go. I know just the place."

I took out my phone to text Callie to let her know I wouldn't be in first period today, and that I would be with Carter. I already know what she's going to say. Can you guess?

We slipped out of the school and headed to the small park nearby, finding a secluded bench under a large oak tree.

"So," I began, "how was the cruise?"

Carter leaned back, a relaxed smile on his face. "It was amazing. The weather was perfect, and the food was incredible. We even went snorkeling."

I nodded, trying to steer the conversation gently. "That sounds great. Did anything interesting happen?"

My phone began to vibrate. I looked at it to see that Callie had responded.

*Knocking boots.*

Yep, I knew it. I turned my attention back to Carter.

He shrugged, looking thoughtful. "Not really. It was mostly just relaxing and hanging out with family. I needed that break."

I bit my lip, deciding to take a more direct approach. "Did you get any mail while you were there? Like a letter or something?"

Carter's eyes flickered with surprise for a brief moment, but he quickly covered it up. "A letter? No, why would I get a letter on a cruise?"

I shrugged, feigning nonchalance. "I don't know. Sometimes hotels or cruise ships deliver mail to the guests. Just curious."

He chuckled, but there was a slight edge to it. "Nope, no letters. Just a lot of sun and sea."

I decided to push a little further. "Well, did anything out of the ordinary happen? You seem a bit... different."

Carter's smile faltered slightly, and he looked away, focusing on the park's playground. "It's just... family stuff. You know how it is."

"Family stuff?" I prompted gently. "Anything you want to talk about?"

He sighed, rubbing the back of his neck. "It's nothing major. Just some things with my mom and her husband. It's been complicated."

I nodded, sensing the tension in his voice. "I get it. Family can be tough."

He looked at me, his eyes searching mine. "What about you? How have things been?"

I hesitated, the events of the weekend flooding back. "It's been... rough."

Carter's expression softened, and he reached out to squeeze my hand. "I'm sorry. Anything *you* want to talk about?" He asked.

I hesitated. I didn't want to tell him anything about the visions yet, nor about my problems at home. Not that I don't trust him, it's just a lot to take in.

"Thanks," I said, appreciating his concern. "It's nothing to major, I'll be okay."

We sat in silence for a moment, the weight of our individual struggles hanging in the air. I wanted to bring up the letter again, to dig deeper, but I didn't want to push him too hard.

"I'm glad we skipped class," Carter said finally, breaking the silence. "It's nice to just talk."

"Yeah," I agreed. "It is."

As the morning sun climbed higher in the sky, I knew this was just the beginning. Eventually, we headed back to school, slipping into the crowd as if we'd been there all along. Carter squeezed my hand one last time before we parted ways, a silent promise that we'd get through this together.

And as I walked to my next class, I spotted Callie giving the biggest grin.

"Hey boot knocker." She snickered.

"Callie shut up." I laughed.

"I can't believe you actually skipped class. Little miss 'always doing the right thing'."

"I just wanted to talk to him." I laughed.

Callie smirked. "You know we should go on a double date. You, Carter, Mike and Me." She said.

Mike is not my favorite person in the world but he makes Callie happy so.

"Sure, we can do that." I smiled.

"Have you seen Josh today?" I asked Callie. "I actually have not." She responded.

Hmm. If he's not in school, I wonder where he is.

The rest of the school day dragged on, my thoughts constantly drifting back to Josh, and my conversation with Carter.

When the final bell rang, I met up with Callie, Mike, and Carter at the front entrance. Callie was already holding Mike's hand, looking happier than ever. Carter approached me, a shy smile playing on his lips.

"Hey." he said softly. "You know.. they don't have to be the only ones who hold hands." he whispered in my ear. The warmth of his breath against my skin, giving me chills.

My heart fluttered, and I nodded, feeling a warmth spread through me as his hand slipped into mine.

We walked together to the nearby McDonald's, the four of us laughing and joking along the way. Callie and Mike led the way, their easy banter setting a light-hearted tone. Carter and I followed, our hands intertwined, a comfortable silence between us.

At McDonald's, we found a booth in the corner and settled in. Callie and Mike sat across from us, their heads close together as they whispered and giggled. Carter and I took our seats, and I couldn't help but feel a little nervous.

As we started eating, Carter turned to me, his eyes earnest. "Caitlyn, I've been wanting to ask you something."

I looked up, my heart pounding. "What is it?"

He took a deep breath, his grip on my hand tightening slightly. "Well we've been talking for a while and I can't shake the feeling inside that I have for you. So I was just wondering, would you be my girlfriend?"

A smile spread across my face, and I felt a rush of happiness. "I thought you'd never ask." I smiled.

His smile mirrored mine, and he leaned in to kiss my cheek. "Whew" He said before pretending to wipe sweat off of his forehead.

We continued eating, the conversation flowing easily. It wasn't long before the topic of the cruise came up again. Callie, ever the curious one, asked, "So, Carter, tell us more about the cruise. Did anything exciting happen?"

Carter shrugged, glancing at me. "Not really. It was just a relaxing trip with the family." He said and they all smiled and nodded.

As we finished our meal, Callie and Mike excused themselves to grab some ice cream. Carter and I stayed at the table, enjoying the quiet moment together.

"Carter," I began, "if there's ever anything you want to talk about, you know you can trust me, right?"

He looked at me, his eyes searching mine. "Is there something you want to ask me?" He asked.

"No, no." I said quickly.

"I just noticed you seem a little distant that's all, like something is on your mind." I added.

He stayed silent for a little.

"Is there something on your mind?" I asked.

"Actually—" Carter started, but before he could finish, Callie and Mike returned to the table, holding ice cream cones.

"We got you guys some ice cream!" Callie squealed, handing us the cones.

"Thank you," Carter and I both said at the same time, smiling at the interruption.

As we enjoyed our ice cream, I couldn't shake the frustration building inside me. Carter was about to say something important, and now the moment was lost. I decided to let it go for now, but I knew I'd have to bring it up again later.

When we finished, we all got up to leave. Callie and Mike headed in one direction, while Carter walked with me towards my house. We strolled in comfortable silence, our hands still intertwined, until we reached the corner where our paths diverged.

"I had a great time today," Carter said, giving my hand a gentle squeeze.

"Me too," I replied, smiling up at him.

"See you tomorrow?" he asked.

"Definitely," I nodded.

He leaned in to give me a kiss, then turned to walk home. I watched him go, feeling a mix of happiness and frustration. As soon as he was out of sight, Callie caught up to me.

"Spill," she demanded, linking her arm with mine.

"What do you mean?" I asked, feigning innocence.

"You've got that look," she said. "Something's on your mind."

I sighed, knowing I couldn't keep it from her any longer. "Okay, let's walk and talk."

We started walking towards my house, and I took a deep breath before diving in. "Remember when I passed out at the park this weekend?"

Callie nodded, her expression turning serious. "Yeah, that was scary. What happened?"

"I had a vision," I said quietly. "Of Carter, on his cruise. He was holding a letter, and he looked really upset."

Callie's eyes widened. "A vision? Like a vision vision?"

I nodded. "Yes, a vision vision. And today, I tried to ask him about it, but he just brushed it off. I know he's hiding something, Callie."

She frowned, thinking. "Maybe it's something personal? Maybe he doesn't know how to talk about it?"

"Maybe," I agreed, "but it's driving me crazy not knowing. I just feel like there's more to it. One thing I have realized with all these visions is that they are showed to me for a reason."

Callie squeezed my arm. "You know, you could try asking him again later. Maybe when it's just the two of you and he's feeling more relaxed."

"Yeah, you're right," I said, appreciating her advice. "Thanks, Callie."

"Anytime," she replied, giving me a reassuring smile. "Just don't stress too much about it. I'm sure he'll open up when he's ready."

As we reached our block, I felt a little lighter. I waved goodbye and headed inside, determined to be patient but also more resolved to get to the bottom of things.

As I walked into the house, I felt a familiar heaviness settle over me. The echoes of last weekend's incident with Steve lingered in my mind, making my skin crawl. I had been avoiding him as much as possible, and now that avoidance was about to be tested.

"Hi, Caitlyn!" my little sister's voice chirped. I managed a smile and walked into the living room. Claire was playing with her toys on the floor.

"Hey, munchkin," I said, ruffling her hair.

Mom and Steve walked in from the kitchen. The sight of Steve made my stomach twist. He gave me a tight-lipped smile that didn't reach his eyes. Mom's gaze was sharp, as always.

"You're late," she said, arms crossed.

"Had some extra studying to do," I lied smoothly, trying to avoid looking at Steve.

"You need to tell us these things, Caitlyn," she scolded. "Dinner's almost ready."

Steve stepped forward, too close for comfort. "We missed you," he said in that oily voice that made my skin crawl.

I swallowed hard, forcing a neutral expression. "I have a lot of homework to finish, so I'll eat later." I said, turning to head upstairs.

"Caitlyn, we need to talk about your attitude." Mom began, but I cut her off.

"Not now, Mom. I have a ton of work." I said firmly, heading for the stairs.

Steve's voice followed me, "You know, Caitlyn, we're here to help if you need it." I heard the sarcasm in his voice.

My heart pounded in my chest, but I didn't turn around. I hurried up the stairs to my room. I closed the door behind me, leaning against it for a moment to catch my breath.

I heard muffled voices from downstairs—Mom and Steve talking, probably about me. I shook my head, trying to shake off the unease, and sat down at my desk. Opening my books, I forced myself to focus on my homework, letting the routine of studying distract me from the tension and fear gnawing at my insides.

As the hours passed, I buried myself in equations and historical dates, finding peace in the predictability of schoolwork. But even as I worked, I knew I couldn't avoid Steve forever. I'd have to find a way to deal with him, and with the visions, and everything else life was throwing at me.

For now, though, I did the only thing I could. I stayed in my room, doing my homework, and tried to hold on to the small moments of peace I could find.

# Chapter 14

A few days had passed, this week blurred by, filled with the usual mix of schoolwork, hanging out with Callie, and stolen moments with Carter.

It was Friday, and the school was buzzing with the usual end-of-week energy. Students were eager to escape to their weekend plans.

As I walked down the nearly empty hallway towards my next class, I noticed a familiar figure leaning against the lockers, staring intently at the floor. It was Josh. Alone, as usual.

"Hey," I said softly, approaching him. "You okay?"

Josh looked up, his eyes widening in surprise. He quickly masked it with a scowl. "What do you want?"

I hesitated for a moment, unsure of how to proceed. "I just wanted to check on you. You seem... not yourself lately."

He snorted. "What are you talking about?"

I took a deep breath, remembering the vision and the incident at the park. "I mean, I know things have been tough at home. I saw what happened at the park with your dad."

Josh's eyes flashed with anger. "You don't know anything about me," he spat, pushing off the lockers and turning away.

"Josh, wait!" I called out, my voice trembling. "Please, just listen."

He stopped but didn't turn around. I took a step closer. "I know you're angry. I would be too. But I couldn't just stand there and do nothing."

Josh slowly turned to face me, his expression a combination of disbelief and curiosity. "You called security. You got him arrested. And now things are even worse at home."

"I'm sorry," I said softly. "I didn't know what else to do. I couldn't let him keep hurting you."

Josh's face softened slightly, but the anger was still there, simmering beneath the surface. "You don't understand what it's like. Now that he's in custody, my mom is a mess. She's blaming me for everything. She's scared he's going to come back and take it out on us even worse."

My heart ached for him. "I'm so sorry, Josh. I never wanted to make things worse for you. I just wanted to help."

He let out a shaky breath, leaning back against the lockers. "I know you meant well, but you don't get it. You can't just fix things with a phone call."

I nodded, feeling the weight of his words. "I get that now. I'm sorry for overstepping. But I absolutely do get it." I said thinking about my own problems.

Josh narrowed his eyes, still defensive. "How could you possibly get it? Your life is perfect compared to mine."

I let out a bitter laugh. "You think my life is perfect? Josh, you have no idea."

He looked taken aback, the anger in his eyes momentarily replaced by curiosity. "What are you talking about?"

I took a deep breath, feeling the knot in my stomach tighten. "My mom... she's an alcoholic. And her boyfriend, Steve, he's... he's not a good guy. He tried to... do things to me the other night. And when I told my mom, she didn't believe me. She sided with him, called me a liar."

Josh's eyes widened in shock, and for a moment, the anger melted away completely. "I... I didn't know."

"Yeah, well, it's not something I like to talk about," I said, my voice trembling.

"But I get it, Josh. I get how messed up things can be at home, and how sometimes you feel trapped and helpless."

Josh's gaze softened, and he looked away, his shoulders slumping. "I didn't know you were going through all that. I just thought... I don't know what I thought honestly."

"I know it's hard to believe," I said. "But we all have our own battles. And sometimes, talking about them can help. You don't have to go through this alone."

Josh sighed, his defenses slowly crumbling. "I just... I don't know how to deal with all this. My dad's always been like this, and now that he's gone, it's like everything's falling apart."

"I'm sorry," I said sincerely. "But maybe now that he's in custody, things can start to get better. Maybe your mom will see that she needs to protect you instead of him."

He shrugged, a hint of hope flickering in his eyes. "Maybe. I just don't know what to do."

"We'll figure it out," I said, offering him a small smile. "You're not alone in this. I'll help you in any way I can."

Josh looked at me, the anger and pain in his eyes slowly giving a hesitant gratitude. "Thanks, Caitlyn. I guess... I guess I needed to hear that."

I nodded, feeling a sense of relief. "Of course,"

"Sorry for being such a dick to you all the time. Well a dick to everyone." He admitted.

"Yeah you definitely have been." I said nodding my head.

He laughed shamefully as he held his head down.

The bell rang, signaling the start of the next class, Josh pushed off the lockers and started to walk away. He paused, looking back at me with newfound respect. "Thanks again, Caitlyn."

I nodded and smiled, watching him disappear down the hallway.

\* \* \*

After school, I decided to take a walk. Callie went somewhere with Mike and Carter had an after school meeting.

I was nearing the park when I saw her again—the old woman who had given me the locket. She was sitting on a bench, her eyes fixed on something in the distance. My heart skipped a beat, and I hesitated for a moment before walking over to her.

She still creeps me out but each time I see her, I feel a little less intimidated.

"Hello," I said softly.

She turned her head slowly and smiled, her eyes warm and knowing.

I sat down next to her, the familiar weight of the locket around my neck feeling heavier than usual. "I've been trying to understand the visions," I admitted. "They're still so confusing."

She nodded slowly, her gaze never leaving mine. Her eyes seemed to hold a world of wisdom and understanding.

I took a deep breath, feeling the knot in my stomach tighten. "Can you help me? Can you maybe show me another one?"

The old woman reached out and gently took my hand. Her touch was warm and reassuring. She didn't say anything, but her eyes conveyed a silent encouragement, urging me to trust in the process.

I closed my eyes, and almost immediately, I felt the world around me shift. When I opened them again, I was in a different place. The air was thick with tension, and I found myself standing in a room. In the center of the room was the same little girl I had seen in the previous vision. She was frantically searching through drawers, her small hands trembling with urgency.

"Where is it?" she whispered to herself, her voice filled with desperation. "I need to find it…"

I watched her, feeling an overwhelming sense of helplessness. What was she looking for? Why was it so important?

Suddenly, the scene shifted again, and I saw a man enter the room. His face was shadowed, but there was something menacing about him. The little girl froze, her eyes wide with fear.

"What are you doing?" he demanded, his voice cold and harsh.

The girl didn't answer, her hands clenching into fists at her sides. The man took a step closer, and I could feel the terror radiating off her.

"Answer me!" he shouted, raising his hand as if he was about to strike her.

And then, just as quickly as it had begun, the vision faded, and I was back on the bench with the old woman. My heart was pounding, and I felt a cold sweat on my forehead.

She squeezed my hand gently, her eyes searching mine for understanding. I nodded, my voice shaky. "Yes… but I still don't understand. Who is she? And what is she looking for?"

The old woman's eyes softened, and she gave a slight nod, as if to say that in time, I would find the answers. She didn't need to speak; her eyes communicated everything.

I looked at her, feeling a mix of frustration and determination. "I just want to help her. I want to understand."

Her gaze reassured me, silently conveying that I would trust in myself and in the visions—they would guide me.

As I walked home, my mind was a whirlwind of thoughts and emotions. The visions were becoming clearer, but they also raised more questions. Who was the little girl? What was she searching for? And how was it all connected to me?

\* \* \*

When I finally reached home, the house was eerily quiet. I walked through the front door, I noticed mom slumped on the couch, tears streaming down her face. She was staring blankly at the television, which was turned off.

"Mom?" I said softly, approaching her. "What's wrong?"

She turned her head slowly, her eyes red and glossy. Her expression hardened as she looked at me. "What do you want now?"

I took a hesitant step closer. "I just wanted to see if you're okay. You look upset."

She snorted, wiping her tears with the back of her hand. "Upset? You think you understand what upset is? You're not the one who's been dealing with this mess."

I tried to offer some comfort. "Dealing with what? Maybe talking about it could help. I'm here for you."

She glared at me with contempt. "Oh, you think you're so perfect, don't you? You don't get to waltz in here and pretend like you care. You've got your own problems. Don't act like you're a saint."

Her words are so dumb sometimes. "I just want to help."

"Help?" she spat. "You can't even help yourself. Just leave me alone. I don't need your pity."

I bit my lip, struggling to keep my composure. "I–"

She turned her back to me, her shoulders trembling as she tried to compose herself. "Just go. I don't want to talk right now."

I stood there for a moment, feeling the weight of her dismissal. My heart ached, but I knew better than to push further. I turned and walked away, heading up to my room, feeling the sting of her words and the emptiness that seemed to follow me everywhere.

I miss her.

I missed the comfort of having a mom who cared. I felt like I hadn't had one since Dad left. Some days were worse than others, and tonight was particularly heavy.

As I sat on my bed, lost in my own thoughts, my phone buzzed on the nightstand. I picked it up and saw Carter's name flashing on the screen. His call came through, and when I answered, his voice was choked with tears.

"Caitlyn?" Carter's voice cracked. "I don't know who else to call. I'm... I'm really worried."

"Carter?" I said, my heart pounding. "What's wrong? Why are you crying?"

"I think my parents are getting a divorce," he sobbed. "When we were on the cruise I found a letter in my stepdad's bag, and it was... it was for another woman. He wrote about missing her, about how he couldn't stop thinking about her."

So that's what the letter said.

My chest tightened. "Oh God, Carter. I'm sorry." I took a deep breath, trying to stay calm for his sake. "Carter, I'm here for you. We'll get through this. I'm so sorry you're dealing with this."

"I just... I don't know who to trust anymore," he said, his voice trembling. "I thought everything was fine, but now... I just don't know."

"They have been arguing non stop, and I don't even think my mom knows about the letters. Should I even tell her?" He asked.

"No, I don't think you should. Not yet at least." I said. If he tells his mom about the letters there's no doubt a divorce would happen.

"Just remember," I said softly, "you're not alone in this. I know things are really tough right now, but we'll find a way through it."

There was a long pause on the other end. "Thanks, Caitlyn. I really needed to hear that."

I could hear the exhaustion in his voice. "Of course. Just relax right now and call me if you need anything, okay?"

"Yeah, I will. Thanks."

After we hung up, I sat there, my thoughts swirling with everything that had happened. Carter's pain felt so familiar, and it made my own struggles seem all the more real.

But for now, I had to focus on being there for Carter.

# Chapter 15

The morning sun peeked through the curtains of my room. I stretched, feeling a mix of anticipation and anxiety for the day ahead. Claire was still sleeping peacefully in her bed, so I decided to get ready and prepare her for the day.

I gently woke Claire and helped her get dressed. "Hey, kiddo, I'm taking you over to Callie's for a little while. She's going to babysit you today."

Claire's sleepy eyes lit up. "Callie's house? Yay!" She loves Callie.

"Just be a good girl and listen to Callie, okay?"

"Okay!" she chirped.

Mom had work today and I wasn't leaving Claire with Steve all day.

Once Claire was ready, I walked her over to Callie's house. Callie greeted us with her usual bright smile and a big hug for Claire. "Hey, Claire! Ready for a fun day?"

Claire nodded eagerly, and I could see the excitement in her eyes.

"Thanks for doing this, Callie." I said sincerely.

"Of course! You know I love spending time with Claire." Callie replied, her gaze softening.

"You go ahead and go knock some boots." Callie said as I rolled my eyes and laughed.

"Never gets old." I said.

I waved goodbye to Claire and headed back to my house as I finished getting ready. Once I was done, I headed out to the nearest bus stop to meet Carter at a cafe.

When I arrived, Carter was already there, sitting at a table by the window, looking a bit distant. I walked over and took a seat across from him. He looked up and managed a small, tired smile.

"Hey," I said, trying to sound cheerful. "How are you holding up?"

He shrugged, his eyes reflecting the exhaustion and worry I had heard in his voice the night before. "I'm getting by. It's been a rough couple of days."

The waiter came by, and we ordered our breakfast. As we waited for our food, Carter stared at the table, his fingers nervously tapping against the surface.

"I can't stop thinking about that letter," Carter said finally. "It's been eating away at me."

I nodded sympathetically. "Do you want to talk about it?"

"Yeah," he said, pulling a folded piece of paper from his pocket and sliding it across the table. "Here it is."

I took the letter, feeling a wave of familiarity as I unfolded it. The handwriting looked strangely familiar, but I couldn't quite place it. The words, however, were clear:

"I'm sorry for leaving. I didn't want to, but I had to. I miss you."

I stared at the letter, trying to make sense of it.

Carter leaned in, his eyes searching mine. "Do you think it means something?"

I continued to read the letter, trying to decipher its meaning. "The letter sounds like it's from someone who's apologizing for leaving and missing the person they wrote it to. But it doesn't explicitly mention a romantic relationship."

Carter frowned. "So you think it might not be for a woman?"

"Maybe," I said thoughtfully.

"So... you think it was for a man?" Carter asked and I busted out laughing.

"No, I mean well.. I don't know." I laughed

"I mean, it could be for anyone. Could it be possible that your stepdad had other children or someone else he was close to?"

Carter shook his head. "No, he didn't have any other kids. It's always been me, my sister and brother. I'm pretty sure he didn't have any other family."

"Are you sure?" I asked, feeling a growing sense of unease. "Is there anyone else in his life who might have been significant?"

Carter thought for a moment. "There's no one I know of. He was always private about his past, but I don't think there's anyone else."

We both sat in silence, the weight of the letter and its implications hanging heavy between us. "It's like a puzzle we can't solve." Carter said, his voice tinged with frustration.

"Yeah," I agreed. "But maybe there's something we're missing. Maybe the letter wasn't meant for someone in his immediate family. It could be someone from his past or someone he had a different kind of relationship with."

Carter looked at me with skepticism. "So, you think there's a chance it's not about a romantic relationship?"

"It's possible," I said. "But we need more information. Maybe there's something else you can find that could give us more context."

We continued to brainstorm, trying to piece together any fragments of information that could help us understand the letter better. As the conversation continued, the cafe's warm ambiance gave comfort.

Finally, as we finished our breakfast, Carter looked a little more at ease. "Thanks for being here. I don't think I can make it through this without you."

"I'm glad I could help." I said, giving him a reassuring smile.

We wrapped up our breakfast, and I couldn't shake some uneasy feeling settling in my chest. I was about to suggest we head out when a familiar, disorienting sensation washed over me.

The cozy cafe and Carter's concerned face began to blur, replaced by the image of a bustling city street. I found myself standing outside a quaint restaurant, its large windows offering a clear view inside.

Through the glass, I saw Mike sitting at a table with a girl who wasn't Callie. The girl was dressed in a stylish, eye-catching outfit, and they were laughing and leaning towards each other. Mike's demeanor was warm and flirtatious, his eyes locked on the girl as he playfully touched her hand.

They shared a private, intimate conversation, their faces close as they exchanged smiles and flirtatious glances. The scene felt like a punch to the gut, and I could almost feel Callie's hurt and betrayal as I watched this moment unfold.

The vision began to fade, pulling me back to the cafe. I blinked, trying to regain my composure. Carter looked up at me, noticing my sudden shift in expression.

"You okay?" he asked concerned.

"Yeah, I'm fine," I said, forcing a smile. "Just... had a moment."

As we left the cafe, I tried to push the vision out of my mind, but the image of Mike and the girl lingered. We walked outside, and as we headed towards the street, I noticed a restaurant across the road with large windows.

My heart raced as we approached. I glanced inside, and there they were—Mike and the girl from my vision, sitting at a table near the window. Mike was laughing at something the girl said, and they looked completely engrossed in each other.

Carter noticed them too and his eyes widened in shock. "Is that... Mike?" he asked, his voice tinged with disbelief.

I nodded, feeling a lump in my throat. "Yeah, it is."

Carter's face fell as he took in the sight. Mike was leaning in, his hand gently brushing the girl's arm as they exchanged flirtatious smiles. The scene from my vision was playing out exactly as I had seen it.

Before we could react, Mike looked up and spotted us. His smile fell and he then looked as if he had just seen a ghost.

"That fucking piece of shit." I said to Carter. I then started walking towards the entrance of the restaurant.

"Oh, you're going in there?" Carter asked but I ignored him as I kept walking.

"Yep you're going in there." He said again.

"Okay we're going in there." He added as he followed me. My steps quickened as I was filled with rage. I already didn't like this son of a bitch and then he goes and cheat on my best friend?

Hell no.

I stormed up to the table, Carter close behind me. Mike's face turned pale as he looked up, trying to find his words.

"So who's this?" I demanded, my voice cold and sharp.

"Oh, uh—this is... uh—she's just a friend," Mike stuttered, glancing nervously at the girl beside him. She looked up with wide eyes, clearly uncomfortable.

"Just a friend?" I scoffed. "That's not what it looks like from where I'm standing."

The girl shifted in her seat, her cheeks flushing. "I didn't know he was with someone," she said softly, avoiding eye contact with me. "I'm really sorry."

"Yeah, you should be sister," I snapped. "And you, Mike, how dare you do this to Callie?"

Mike's eyes darted between me and Carter, who stood beside me with a stern expression. "Caitlyn, this isn't what it looks like," Mike tried to explain, his voice shaking. "I didn't mean for it to happen like this."

"Not what it looks like?" I shot back. "You're sitting here flirting with another girl while Callie thinks you're being faithful. How is that not exactly what it looks like?"

Mike opened his mouth, but no words came out. He looked at the girl next to him, who now had a look of regret on her face.

"Did you really think you could get away with this?" Carter interjected, his voice low but intense. "You were caught red-handed, Mike. There's no excuse."

Mike's face twisted with anger and embarrassment. "You know what? This isn't any of your business," he snapped, glaring at both Carter and me. "You two think you're so perfect, but you don't know the first thing about what's going on in my life. Just stay out of it."

Carter's jaw clenched, but before he could respond, I stepped in front of him, my eyes blazing with fury. "You think you can just brush us off? This is my best friend's life you're fucking with. You're the one who made it our business."

Mike sneered, his gaze shifting back to me. "And what, you're gonna lecture me now? You're just some high school kid playing detective. You don't get to dictate how I live my life."

I took a step closer, my voice rising with every word. "And what the hell are you? You're nothing but a coward hiding behind excuses."

Mike's face flushed with anger. "Oh, please. Like you've never screwed up before? Don't act so righteous. You've got your own messes to deal with."

I narrowed my eyes, feeling my anger boil over. "You don't get to deflect your mistakes onto us. And don't you dare try to turn this around. We're here because we care about Callie, something you clearly don't understand. So, get your head out of your ass and face the consequences of your actions."

Mike then got up and took a step towards me with his fist clenched. Carter got in front of me, shielding me with his whole body.

"I suggest you back up bro." Carter said firmly.

Mike's face was a mask of fury as he clenched his fists harder and took a step toward Carter. "You think you can intimidate me?" Mike spat, his voice dripping with venom. "You don't know who you're messing with."

Carter stood his ground, his posture rigid and defensive. "I'm not here to fight, Mike. But if you want to act like a thug, then go ahead and try me."

Mike's anger flared as he threw a punch, aiming for Carter's face. Carter dodged the swing, his reflexes sharp. In a swift move, Carter's hand shot out, grabbing Mike's wrist and twisting it behind his back.

"Back off, Mike," Carter growled, his grip tightening. "This isn't the way to handle this."

Mike struggled against Carter's hold, his face contorted with rage. "Let me go" Mike said.

"You're going to stop acting like a child and deal with the mess you've made." Carter said.

Mike tried to wrench free, but Carter's hold was firm.

"Let him go, Carter," I said, my voice steady despite the adrenaline coursing through me. "We've made our point. There's no need to escalate things further."

With a final, frustrated grunt, Mike yanked his arm away from Carter's grip and stormed out of the restaurant, slamming the door behind him. The girl he'd been with hurriedly followed, casting a final, remorseful glance back before disappearing through the door.

Carter exhaled deeply, his shoulders relaxing as he released the tension in his body. "Are you okay?" he asked, turning to me with concern.

I nodded, though my heart was still racing. "Yeah, I'm fine. Thanks for stepping in. I couldn't have handled that on my own."

"I wont let anyone hurt you, not if I'm present". He said and I gave a soft smile.

We left the restaurant and as we walked back towards Callie's house, the reality of what had just happened began to sink in. I don't know how

I'm going to tell her. This is going to break her I already know.

"Thanks for having my back today. But, um, I think I need to handle this next part on my own." I said as we reached Callie's house.

Carter looked at me. "Are you sure? I can stay with you if you need me."

I shook my head, offering him a small, appreciative smile. "No, I think I need to do this alone."

Carter nodded, giving me a reassuring pat on the shoulder. "Alright. Call me if you need anything."

With a final nod, I watched as Carter walked away, heading toward his home. I took a deep breath, trying to steady myself before approaching Callie's house.

As I entered, Claire ran up to me with her usual enthusiasm. "Caitlyn! I missed you!"

I scooped her up into a hug. "I missed you too, Claire. How was your morning with Callie?"

"It was so much fun!" Claire said, her eyes sparkling with excitement. "We played games and had Twinkies!" She screamed.

Callie has gotten her addicted to Twinkies.

I smiled, relieved to see her happy. "That's great. You've had a good time then."

Claire nodded and continued to tell me about her adventures with Callie as we walked toward the living room. Callie was sitting on the couch, her eyes lighting up when she saw us.

"Hey, Caitlyn," Callie greeted warmly. "How was breakfast?"

"Hey," I said, trying to keep my voice steady. "It was... eventful. Listen, there's something I need to tell you. It's important."

Callie's smile faded slightly, her expression turning serious. "What's up?"

I took a deep breath, trying to find the right words. "I saw Mike today. He was with another girl. They were... close. It wasn't just a friendly meet-up."

Callie looked at me with pain. "You saw him with someone else?"

I nodded. "I'm really sorry, Callie. I didn't know how to break this to you, but you needed to know."

To my surprise, Callie's shoulders slumped, and she looked down, a defeated expression on her face. "I knew."

What?

"You knew?"

Callie nodded, her voice barely a whisper. "I had a feeling something was off. I saw them together a few times, and I tried to ignore it. I... I was afraid to be alone, so I stayed with him, hoping things would get better."

"Oh, Callie," I said softly, moving closer to her.

"It's okay," Callie said, her voice trembling. "I just didn't want to be alone with the truth. I kept hoping it was just a misunderstanding."

I reached out and took Callie's hand, giving it a reassuring squeeze. "Can I be honest with you?" I asked and she nodded her head.

"Are you fucking serious?" I said and her eyes widened. "Are you seriously telling me that my best friend—who is basically the most beautiful, amazing girl on the planet—was actually trying to stick around with a guy who's clearly failing a relationship audit?" I said, frustration in my voice.

Callie looked at me with wide eyes, surprised. "I didn't know you felt that way."

"Of course you didn't," I said, rolling my eyes. "Because you were busy being a saint in denial. Listen, Callie, you've got to see your own worth. You're not a fucking backup plan."

Callie's eyes filled with tears, but she managed a small, grateful smile. "I needed to hear that, even if it's a bit harsh."

"Harsh?" I said, chuckling softly. "Let's just say I'm saving my gentler approach for when you start dating someone who doesn't have a wandering eye."

"And as long as you got me, you will never be alone." I said as Callie smiled.

Claire, sensing the tension, looked up with wide eyes. "Callie okay?"

Callie forced a smile and crouched down to Claire's level. "I'm okay, baby. Just a little sad right now."

Claire wrapped her arms around Callie, offering her a comforting hug. Callie's smile grew a bit more genuine as she hugged Claire back.

I felt a pang of sadness for Callie, but also a sense of relief that the truth was out. It was going to be a long road ahead, but she wasn't alone. I promised myself I would be by her side every step of the way.

"Do you want some company or do you want to be alone?" I asked.

"Your company would be nice." She smiled. I smiled back and I got up and headed to the kitchen. I grabbed a box of Twinkies and took them out to Callie.

Her eyes lit up.

"See, when you find a guy who looks up at you the way you look at Twinkies, you'll know they are the one." I said and she laughed loudly.

"Yeah you're right about that."

# Chapter 16

I spent a few hours with Callie, making sure she was okay. We did what we usually always do when we hang out, watch movies, gossip and eat junk.

"What time does your mom get home?" Callie asked as she paused the movie we were watching.

"Not until late tonight, she's doing a double, thank God." I said and she laughed. "Why?" I asked.

"I think you should invite Carter over to your house. You deserve a nice boot knocking session." She said.

"Oh my God, you know we haven't done anything and I highly doubt we will anytime soon." I said laughing.

"You never know," She said. "Come on invite him and go home. Make sure your room is all clean and shit." She added.

I thought about it for a minute. "Steve might be there." I said rolling my eyes. Callie went and looked out of the living room window, and looked down at my house.

"Well his car is gone. So get up" She said. "I'll watch Claire just go have fun." She said as I looked at Claire who had fallen asleep on the couch.

"Fine." I said smiling. I got up and called Carter as I headed out of Callie's house and back to my own.

"Hey, you okay?" Carter asked as he answered the phone.

"Yes I'm okay. I wanted to see if you would want to come over to my house to just...hang?" I asked nervously.

"Of course, what time?" He asked. I took the phone off of my ear to check the time.

"Uh, give me about 30 minutes." I said. "Gotcha, see you soon." He said as he hung up the phone.

I sped walk to my house, walking in and started to clean as much as I can. I then went inside of my room and changed into some sweats and a plain buttoned shirt.

Carter had texted me saying he was on his way over. I grabbed some perfume, sprayed it more than I probably should have, and headed downstairs.

The doorbell rang, I opened the door and there he was. I felt my heart began to race, this boy just gets me going.

"Hey, come on in." I said welcoming him into my house.

"Thank you, nice place." He said.

We went upstairs and into my room. He started to look around, observing the little things like my posters, and wall art, and making comments on them.

I put on some soft music, and the gentle melody filled the room, creating a calm and inviting atmosphere. We were sitting on my bed, talking about everything and nothing.

"You know, today was a lot," Carter said, looking at me with those deep, earnest eyes of his.

"Tell me about it," I replied, letting out a small laugh. "I feel like I've been on an emotional roller coaster."

He reached out and took my hand, his touch warm and reassuring. "How is Callie?" He asked.

"She's good. Callie is strong, she won't let something like this hold her down." I said as he smiled.

"I wanted to thank you again for helping me through all this, you know with my stepdad and everything. Don't think I would have managed without you." He spoke.

I squeezed his hand gently. "You would have managed. You're stronger than you think."

He smiled, a shy, sweet smile that made my heart flutter. "I don't know about that. But I do know that having you here makes everything better."

There was a moment of silence, a comfortable, lingering silence where words weren't necessary. Carter's gaze met mine, and I felt a connection, a pull that was undeniable.

"There is just something about you," he said, his voice soft and sincere. "Today, seeing how much you care, how much you're willing to do for the people you love... it made me realize just how much you mean to me."

My heart skipped a beat. "Carter..."

He leaned in slowly, giving me plenty of time to pull away if I wanted to. But I didn't. Instead, I closed the distance between us, our lips meeting in a gentle, tender kiss. It was soft at first, a tentative exploration, but then it deepened, growing more passionate as we let go of our inhibitions.

As we kissed, the world outside faded away. It was just the two of us, wrapped up in this moment of pure connection. His hands moved to my waist, pulling me closer, and I felt a warmth spread through me, a warmth that chased away the lingering shadows of doubt and fear.

We pulled back slightly, breathless but smiling. "Wow," Carter whispered, his forehead resting against mine. "That was... incredible."

"Yeah," I agreed, my voice barely more than a whisper. "It was."

He cupped my face in his hands, his thumbs brushing gently against my cheeks. I felt a rush of emotions. Our lips met again, this time with more urgency, more need. We fell back onto the bed, our bodies entwined as we explored this new feeling. Every touch, every kiss, was a revelation, a promise of the connection we shared.

Carter's hands moved with a deliberate slowness, unbuttoning my shirt and sliding it off my shoulders. I followed his lead, my fingers trembling slightly as I undid his. The feeling of his skin against mine sent shivers down my spine, a mixture of anticipation and excitement.

"Are you sure?" he whispered, his voice husky with desire.

"Yes," I replied, my voice steady. "I'm sure."

We moved together, shedding the last of our clothes and exploring each other with a new intensity. His touch was gentle, yet filled with passion, and I felt my breath hitch as he kissed a trail down my neck. We took our time, savoring every moment, every sensation.

When we finally came together, it was with a sense of rightness, of belonging. The world outside ceased to exist as we moved in sync, our bodies and souls connected in a way I had never experienced before. It was more than just physical; it was an expression of everything we felt for each other, a bond that went beyond words.

As we lay together afterward, wrapped in each other's arms, peace washed over me. I felt complete, loved, and cherished in a way I had never imagined. In a way that I have never felt.

Carter rose up just a pinch and grabbed my face, caressing my cheek. He stared into my eyes, causing the butterflies in my stomach to go violently crazy.

"I love you." he said. My heart sped up as I digested those three words. I haven't heard I love you from anyone except Callie in so long. I didn't think I was even capable of being loved like this. I was scared to say it back though. I have a habit of loving people harder and more than they love me.

But with Carter, something just felt different. I felt like I could love him without feeling like the energy wouldn't be reciprocated. I let out a shaky breath.

"I love you too." I said. He began to kiss me again.

"Caitlyn!" Steve's voice roared through the house.

My heart stopped. Carter and I quickly pulled apart, scrambling to cover ourselves. But it was too late. Steve burst into my room, his face red with anger.

"What the hell is going on here?" he yelled, his eyes blazing as he took in the scene.

"Steve, get out!" I shouted, trying to shield myself with the blanket.

"You little whore!" he screamed, lunging towards Carter. "Get out of my house!"

Carter tried to reason with him. "Woah, okay. We didn't mean—"

But Steve wasn't listening. He grabbed Carter by the arm and yanked him off the bed, practically throwing him towards the door. "Get out! Now!"

Carter stumbled but regained his balance. He looked back at me, worry etched across his face.

"Just go," I mouthed.

Carter hesitated, then nodded and hurried out of the room. Steve turned his fury back on me, his face twisted with rage.

"How dare you bring a boy into my house and defile it like this!" he yelled.

"This isn't your house," I shot back, my fear quickly turning to anger. "You came here and took over! This is my mom's house!"

Steve's eyes narrowed, and for a moment, I saw a dangerous glint in them. "You think you can talk to me like that? After what I just saw?"

I stood my ground, my voice shaking but defiant. "Yes, I can. Because you have no right to—"

Before I could finish, Steve lunged at me. His hand connected with my cheek, sending a sharp pain through my face. I stumbled back, my vision blurring.

"Don't you ever talk back to me!" he snarled, advancing on me again.

"Get away from me!" I screamed, trying to back away.

Steve grabbed my arm, his grip tight and painful. "You need to learn your place, little girl."

I struggled against him, my mind racing. Summoning every ounce of strength, I managed to twist out of his grasp and ran for the door.

Steve was right behind me, his footsteps heavy and menacing. "Get your ass back here!" Steve bellowed as he closed in on me.

I darted down the hallway, heart pounding in my chest, and burst into the kitchen. I scanned the room for something, anything to defend myself with. My eyes landed on a heavy frying pan hanging by the stove. Without a second thought, I grabbed it and spun around to face him.

Steve halted, eyes wide with surprise and anger. "Put that down, Caitlyn," he ordered, but there was a slight tremor in his voice.

"Stay away from me!" I shouted, brandishing the pan.

Steve took a step forward, and I swung the pan with all my might, just missing him as he ducked back. "You little bitch," he spat, recovering quickly and lunging at me again.

I swung the pan again, this time connecting with his shoulder. Steve let out a pained grunt, staggering back. Taking advantage of his momentary disorientation, I ran for the front door. Steve caught up to me quick before I can escape. He grabbed my arm and yanked me back into the house.

"Where do you think you're going?" he hissed, his grip tightening painfully on my arm.

"Let me go!" I screamed, struggling against him. But Steve was much stronger than me, and his hold was like iron.

"Shut up!" he snarled, dragging me towards the living room. He threw me onto the couch, and I landed hard, the wind knocked out of me. Before I could recover, he was on top of me, his hands pinning me down.

"You think you can just do whatever you want in my house?" he growled, his face inches from mine. "You think you can disrespect me and get away with it?"

"Get off me!" I cried, trying to push him away. But he was too strong, his weight pressing me into the couch.

"I said you need to learn your place," he said, his voice low and menacing. He grabbed the collar of my shirt and ripped it open, the buttons flying off in all directions.

"No! Stop!" I shouted, panic flooding through me. I kicked and thrashed, trying to free myself, but it was no use. Steve's hands were everywhere, his touch making my skin crawl.

"Stop fighting," he ordered, his breath hot and foul against my face. "You're only making it worse for yourself."

I twisted and turned, desperate to get away, but his grip was unyielding. I felt his hand slide up my thigh, and a cold wave of terror washed over me.

"Please," I begged, tears streaming down my face. "Don't do this."

Steve ignored my pleas, his eyes dark with lust and anger. "You brought this on yourself," he said, his voice a twisted mockery of sympathy. "You need to be taught a lesson."

Summoning every ounce of strength, I kneed him hard in the groin. Steve let out a strangled cry of pain, his grip loosening as he doubled over. Seizing the opportunity, I pushed him off me and scrambled to my feet.

Without looking back, I ran out of the house as fast as I could. My heart pounded in my chest, fear driving me forward. I burst through Callie's front door, gasping for breath.

"Caitlyn, what happened?" Callie asked, rushing over to me.

"Steve... he tried to..." I couldn't finish the sentence, tears streaming down my face.

"Oh my God," Callie said, her eyes wide with horror. She pulled me into a tight hug. "You're safe now. You're safe, breathe."

"We need to call the police," I managed to say, my voice shaking.

"Absolutely," Callie agreed, already reaching for her phone. "Stay here, I'll take care of everything."

As Callie called the police, I sat on the couch, trembling. Claire stirred from her sleep and looked up at me with sleepy eyes.

"Cait? What's wrong?" she asked, rubbing her eyes.

"Nothing, Claire," I said, trying to keep my voice calm. "Everything's going to be okay."

A few minutes later, Callie hung up the phone and came back to me. "The police are on their way," she said, sitting down beside me and taking my hand.

"What happened?" She asked. I explained the whole situation to Callie while we waited for the police.

"I can't keep going through this Callie, Steve has to go. I will not let him keep doing this. And I'm worried for Claire. If he touches her I swear to God I will fucking kill him. I will." I said beginning to cry.

Callie held my hand tighter. "That's not going to happen. Everything will be okay." She said.

As Callie and I sat on the couch, she kept a comforting hand on mine, trying to reassure me that everything would be okay. Suddenly, the doorbell rang. Callie got up to answer it and returned with Carter by her side.

"Caitlyn!" Carter rushed over to me, his face etched with worry. "Are you okay? What happened?"

I stood up and hugged him tightly, feeling the safety of his arms around me. "I'm okay now," I whispered, my voice trembling. "But Steve... he tried to..."

"I'm going to beat the shit out of him," Carter growled, his eyes darkening with rage.

"No, Carter," I said, pulling back and looking up at him. "It won't help. The police are on their way. Let them handle it."

He clenched his fists but nodded reluctantly, his jaw tight. "Fine. But if he ever comes near you again, I won't hold back."

The sound of sirens grew louder, and moments later, the police arrived. Callie opened the door for them and explained the situation briefly. The officers took our statements and reassured me that they would handle Steve.

Callie, Carter, Claire, and I followed the police back to my house. When we arrived, I was horrified to see my mom standing on the porch, her face a mask of fury. She must have come home early from work.

"What the hell is going on here?" she demanded as we approached.

"Mom, Steve tried to... he tried to assault me," I said, my voice breaking.

My mom's eyes narrowed. "You're doing this shit again Caitlyn?"

"I'm not! He tried to—"

"Enough!" she shouted, cutting me off. She turned to the police. "I'm sorry, officers. My daughter has a tendency to overreact. She's always causing trouble and making things up."

The officers looked at me sympathetically. "Ma'am, we need to take this seriously. Your daughter is clearly distressed."

"She's lying!" my mom insisted, her voice cold. "She's always been a liar."

"Mom, please! You have to believe me," I pleaded, tears streaming down my face.

"Caitlyn, go to your room," she ordered, her tone leaving no room for argument.

Carter stepped forward, anger flashing in his eyes. "You can't just ignore this. She's telling the truth!"

My mom glared at him. "And who the hell are you? This is a family matter."

The police officers intervened, their voices firm. "Ma'am, we need to investigate this properly. We'll need to speak with both you and your daughter separately."

Reluctantly, my mom nodded, and the officers led us inside. They took my statement again in more detail while another officer spoke with my mom.

"Do you have somewhere you can stay tonight?" one of the officers asked me gently after we finished.

I glanced at Callie, who immediately nodded. "She can stay with me."

"Thank you," the officer said. "We'll ensure that Steve is taken into custody. You're safe now, Caitlyn."

As we left the house, I couldn't believe my mom had sided with Steve again.

We headed back to Callie's house, Claire was with me still. I couldn't even look at my mom or that house right now. Carter had gone on home for the night, promising me he would call me in the morning.

"Are you okay?" Callie asked me as we entered her house. I nodded my head. She then went and got some blankets from her linen closet and we all camped out in the living room.

"It's been a rough day huh?" She asked and I took a deep breath.

"Sure has." I said.

"Well.." Callie started. "Something good did come out of today." She said and I couldn't even think back because of how foggy my brain was at the moment.

"What?" I asked. "You knocked some boots." She said and we both started laughing.

"Oh yeah!" I said

"Oh my God Callie, I'm a boot knocker." I laughed

"I know that's right."

Callie and I laughed together, the humor of the moment breaking through the heaviness that had been weighing us down. It felt good to laugh, to find a bit of light in such a dark day.

# Chapter 17

The next morning, I woke up to the smell of pancakes and the sound of Callie bustling around in the kitchen. Claire was still asleep, her small form curled up under the blankets. I gently extricated myself and made my way to the kitchen.

"Morning," Callie greeted me with a warm smile. "I thought we could all use a good breakfast."

"Thanks, Callie," I said, feeling a pang of gratitude. "You're amazing, you know that?"

She waved me off. "It's what best friends are for. Now, sit down and eat."

As we ate, I felt a sense of normalcy returning, a fragile semblance of routine. The pancakes were warm and comforting, a stark contrast to the turmoil of the previous night.

After breakfast, I decided to call Carter. He said he would call me but I couldn't wait, I needed to hear his voice, to feel that connection again. He answered on the first ring.

"Hey," he said, his voice filled with concern. "How are you holding up?"

"I'm okay," I replied, feeling a bit more steady with each passing moment. "Thank you for everything last night. I don't know what I would have done without you."

"You don't have to thank me," he said gently. "I'm just glad you're safe. Do you want to meet up later?"

"Yes, I'd like that," I said, feeling a sense of relief. "I need to get out of the house for a bit."

"Okay, I'll come pick you up around noon," he said. "Hey, how would you feel about coming over to my house? Maybe meeting my people?" He asked and I could feel the nerves starting up.

"Uh- yeah, sure, of course." I said.

"Great! Okay I'll see you soon." he said.

After we hung up, I helped Callie clean up the kitchen. "Carter wants me to meet his family." I spilled to Callie as I washed the dishes.

"Oh my gosh, that's a big step!" She exclaimed.

"Is it normal to be this nervous? I mean what if they hate me? Or think I look like a frog or something." I admitted and Callie laughed.

I stared at her to let her know I was serious. "Oh come on Caitlyn, have you seen yourself? You're like barbie just human form, and a bit darker." She laughed.

"Ugh." I groaned. "Okay I'll just go." I said.

"They will love you and if they don't they're stupid, or blind, or both." She said and I smiled. "Okay thanks Callie." I said continuing to clean the same dish I had been cleaning for a few minutes.

"I think it's clean." Callie said pointing to the plate.

"Oh." I giggled.

After cleaning the kitchen I took a shower, letting the hot water wash away some of the tension. I dressed in comfortable clothes and spent some time playing with Claire, trying to distract her from everything that had happened.

As noon approached, I felt a mixture of anticipation and anxiety. I was eager to see Carter, but the events of the previous night still loomed large in my mind. When the doorbell rang, my heart skipped a beat.

"I'll get it," Callie said, giving me an encouraging smile.

She opened the door to reveal Carter, who looked as handsome and reassuring as ever. He stepped inside and pulled me into a tight hug.

"Hey," he said softly. "How are you doing?"

"Better now," I admitted, holding onto him.

Callie watched us with a knowing smile. "You two take care of each other, okay?"

"We will," Carter promised, giving her a grateful nod.

"My mom let me use her car today." He said and I smiled widely. I get to see him drive. I could barely focus though because my mind was still on meeting his family.

As we walked towards the car, I took a deep breath. "Carter, can I ask you something?"

"Of course," he said, looking at me with concern.

"Can we maybe meet your family another day? I'm just not mentally prepared right now."

He nodded immediately, his eyes softening. "Absolutely. We don't have to do anything you're not ready for. How about we go to the beach instead? Just the two of us."

Relief washed over me. "That sounds perfect."

We drove to the beach, enjoying the peacefulness of each other's company. When we arrived, we kicked off our shoes and walked along the shoreline, the cool sand beneath our feet and the sound of waves crashing against the shore.

We spent the afternoon making sandcastles, playing in the water, and laughing. For the first time in a while, I felt truly happy and carefree. As the sun began to dip towards the horizon, casting a golden hue over the ocean, I looked around and then noticed the old woman standing a little way off.

"I need to use the bathroom," I told Carter, pointing to the nearby facilities. "I'll be right back."

He nodded, his face content. "Okay. I'll be here."

I made my way towards the old woman with anticipation. She greeted me with a warm smile.

"Hi," I said, my voice trembling slightly. "You're here again."

She nodded her head and reached out her hand for me to grab indicating that there was something she had to show me.

I nodded, knowing that whatever she had to show me was important. She took my hand, her grip strong, and suddenly, the world around me began to blur.

I was back in the familiar surroundings of the vision, the little girl with the golden locket standing before me. This time, the vision was clearer, more detailed. The girl was running through a dense forest, her laughter echoing through the trees. She looked happy, carefree, her eyes sparkling with joy.

As she ran, I saw a woman standing by a stream, her back turned towards us. The girl approached her, tugging on her dress. The woman turned, revealing a kind, gentle face that bore a striking resemblance to the old woman. She knelt down and embraced the girl, their bond palpable.

The scene shifted, and I saw the girl in a quaint little house, sitting by a fireplace with the woman. The woman was telling her stories, their laughter filling the room. There was a sense of warmth, of love, that permeated the air.

Then, the vision grew darker. The girl was older now, and the woman was frail, lying in a bed. The girl held the woman's hand, tears streaming down her face. The woman whispered something to her, pressing the golden locket into her hand before closing her eyes for the last time.

The vision faded, and I was back on the beach, the old woman still holding my hand. Her eyes were filled with sadness and understanding.

"That girl was you," I said softly.

She nodded. "And the woman was your mother." I said, she nodded again.

"Was the locket hers as well?" I asked and she nodded her head yes.

I felt a lump form in my throat. "Why did you give it to me?"

"Because you have the strength to bear it, to understand it, and to use it for good," she said finally speaking again.

"It's in your blood." She said as she began to walk away.

In my blood? Huh? I was even more confused than usual but I brushed it off for the time being.

As she faded from view, I made my way back to Carter.

When I reached Carter, he looked at me with concern. "Are you okay?"

I nodded, a small smile on my lips. "Yeah, I'm okay."

He took my hand, his touch comforting. "Let's stay here a little longer. Just you and me."

I agreed, feeling nothing but pure tranquility. We sat down on a large beach towel and watched the waves for a while in silence. Then Carter turned to me, his expression serious.

"Caitlyn, what are you going to do about Steve and your mom?" he asked gently.

I sighed, the weight of his question pressing down on me. "I don't know, Carter. I feel like I should do something, but it's so complicated."

He squeezed my hand. "I get that. But you can't just keep living like this. It's not healthy for you or Claire."

"I know," I admitted. "But confronting my mom... it's not easy. She's been like this for so long, and I don't think she wants to change."

"Maybe it's not about changing her," Carter said thoughtfully. "Maybe it's about protecting yourself and Claire. Finding a way to create a safe space for both of you."

I nodded slowly. "You're right. I need to figure out a way to do that. But it's hard to know where to start."

"I'm here for you," he said, his eyes full of determination.

Tears welled up in my eyes, but this time they were tears of gratitude. "Thank you."

He leaned in to kiss me and we sat there, holding hands and watching the waves, knowing that while the road ahead was uncertain, we had each other to lean on. And for now, that was enough.

# Chapter 18

C laire and I had been staying with Callie and her family for a few days, but I decided that it was time to go back home before we overstay our welcome. Of course Callie said we didn't have to, but I insisted.

The walk home felt heavy with anticipation and dread. I held Claire's hand tightly as we walked up to the front door, the familiar creak of the porch boards under our feet amplifying my anxiety. Callie had offered to come with us, but I insisted on facing this alone.

As we stepped inside, the house felt colder, emptier. Claire's grip on my hand tightened.

"Mom?" I called out, my voice trembling slightly.

From the kitchen, Mom appeared, her face set in a hard, angry expression. She looked at us, her eyes narrowing. "You're back," she said flatly.

I nodded, swallowing hard. "Where's Steve?"

Her jaw clenched, and she took a deep breath, as if trying to hold back a flood of emotions. "He moved out," she said finally, her voice laced with anger.

I blinked in surprise. "He did? Why?" I asked but in the inside pure joy took over.

"Because he can't be around you by court law," she snapped, her eyes blazing.

"They issued a restraining order after your little stunt. He can't come near you, which means he can't stay here."

Relief washed over me. I had done this to protect Claire and myself. "Mom, I... I had to do it. He was dangerous."

"Dangerous?" she repeated, her voice rising. "He was the only stability we had! And now he's gone because of you!"

I felt my heart sink. "Mom, you don't understand—"

"Don't I?" she interrupted, stepping closer. "Do you have any idea what you've done to this family? You've ruined everything, Caitlyn!"

I took a deep breath, trying to stay calm. "Mom, he was hurting us. I did what I had to do to keep us safe."

Her face twisted with rage. "Safe? You think we're safe now? We aren't safe!"

"Mom, please," I pleaded. "We can get through this together. We don't need him."

She shook her head, tears of fury in her eyes. "I wish your father had taken you with him when he left," she spat. "There is so many things in life that I regret, but having you for a daughter tops it all."

The words hit me like a physical blow, knocking the wind out of me. Claire whimpered beside me, her small body trembling.

"Mom," I whispered, my voice breaking. "How can you say that?"

"Because it's true," she said coldly. "You've been nothing but a burden. Your father knew it, and I know it too. I wish you were gone."

Tears streamed down my face as I struggled to find words. "Well I'm sorry you feel that way," I said finally. "But I'm not going anywhere. Claire needs me, and I'll do whatever it takes to protect her."

"Protect her from what?" she scoffed. "From me?"

"From anyone who tries to hurt her," I said, my voice steady despite the tears. "Even if that includes you."

Her eyes blazed with anger, but she said nothing. I turned to Claire, who was clutching my hand tightly. "Come on, Claire. Let's go to your room."

We walked past Mom, who stood there, seething, as we made our way down the hallway. Inside our room, I closed the door and knelt down in front of Claire.

"Are you okay?" I asked gently.

She nodded, her eyes wide and scared. "I'm scared."

I hugged her tightly. "I know. But we're going to be okay. I promise."

As I held her, I felt a resolve harden within me. No matter what Mom said or did, I would protect Claire.

After a while, Claire fell asleep in my arms, and I gently laid her down on the bed. I sat there, watching her sleep, and felt a sudden wave of exhaustion wash over me. I closed my eyes for just a moment, and that's when it happened.

The vision took hold, pulling me into a different time and place. I saw my mom, younger and happier, standing in a sunlit kitchen. She was laughing, a sound I hadn't heard in years. There was a man beside her, his face obscured, but his presence warm and loving.

The scene shifted, and I saw her crying alone in the dark, a bottle of wine in her hand. The man was gone, and she was screaming into the emptiness, her pain intense. I wanted to reach out to her, to comfort her, but I was just an observer, powerless to change anything.

Then, I saw a memory I'd almost forgotten: my mom holding me as a little girl, singing softly as she rocked me to sleep. Her eyes were full of love and tenderness, a stark contrast to the woman she had become.

The vision faded, leaving me with a deep sense of sorrow. I know that she's like this because of dad leaving. I don't understand why she has to act like this towards me though.

When I opened my eyes, I was back in our room, Claire still asleep beside me. I wiped away the tears that had fallen during the vision and took a deep breath.

I just want her back.

# Chapter 19

I felt excited and nervous as I walked up to Carter's house for the first time. It's been a little over a week since we last talked about this, and we decided on this weekend. I'd been to his neighborhood before, but meeting his family was a big step. Carter opened the door with a warm smile and welcomed me inside.

"Hey, Caitlyn! Come on in. Mom's in the kitchen, and the rest of the crew is around here somewhere," Carter said.

"I'm so nervous," I replied.

"Don't be. They'll love you," he said. "My stepdad is at work right now, but he should be here a little later," he added.

As we walked in, Carter's mom, a kind-looking woman with an infectious smile, came out of the kitchen.

"You must be Caitlyn! I've heard so much about you. I'm Carter's mom. It's so nice to finally meet you," she said.

"It's nice to meet you too, Mrs. Hart," I responded.

"Oh, call me Colleen," she smiled.

"Okay," I chuckled.

Just then, a little boy darted into the room, followed by an older girl.

"This is my little brother, Tommy, and my older sister, Kayla," Carter introduced.

"Hi!" Tommy grinned.

"Hey, Caitlyn. Welcome to the madhouse," Kayla said, smiling.

I laughed, feeling more at ease with the friendly atmosphere. We all sat down in the living room, chatting about school and summer plans.

"So, how did you two meet? Carter never really explained all of that," Kayla asked.

"Oh, uh, we actually met at the store. I was shopping for something and he was the cashier at the time," I said, thinking back to when we first met.

"Ah, he turned on his charm and swept you off your feet, I see," she said, and I blushed.

"Okay, anyways," Carter laughed, trying to change the subject.

"How about we look through some old family photos? I've got albums full of embarrassing pictures of Carter," Colleen suggested.

"Mom, no! That's not necessary," Carter blushed.

"Oh, come on, Carter! It'll be fun. I'd love to see them," I teased.

Carter sighed but relented. Colleen brought out a few photo albums and placed them on the coffee table. We began flipping through the pages, laughing at old photos of Carter in various stages of his childhood.

"You were such a cute baby, Carter!" I giggled.

"Oh, what? I'm not cute anymore?" he asked.

"You're more than cute now," I whispered softly, winking as he began to blush a bit.

"Look at this one. Carter had the chicken pox for the first time," Kayla said, pointing to a picture of Carter covered in red marks.

Carter groaned, hiding his face behind a pillow. As we continued looking through the pictures, my eyes landed on a peculiar photo. It was a picture of different kinds of beans arranged to spell out "I love you."

"This is interesting. Where did this come from?" I asked, frowning.

"No idea. I don't remember that at all," Carter peeked over.

I stared at the photo, a strange familiarity tugging at the edges of my memory. Suddenly, a vivid flashback hit me.

I was five years old, sitting at the kitchen table with my mom. We were surrounded by bowls of different kinds of beans: black beans, pinto beans, kidney beans. My mom, her face gentle and warm, was helping me spell out words with the beans on a large piece of construction paper.

"Look, Mom, I made an 'I'!" I said excitedly, placing a line of black beans in front of me.

The memory faded, leaving me staring at the photo in Carter's album, confused. I shrugged it off and continued flipping through the pages. We laughed at more baby pictures of Carter, and Colleen excused herself to check on dinner.

"Enjoying the baby photos, Caitlyn?" Kayla smirked.

"Absolutely. These are gold," I grinned as I looked at Carter who playfully rolled his eyes.

An hour passed, filled with delicious food and lively conversation. Colleen's cooking was amazing, and I felt a warm sense of belonging as we all shared stories and jokes around the table. As dinner wound down, Colleen suggested we go through more photos.

"How about we continue looking through the albums? I've got plenty more to show you," Colleen said, smiling.

"Sure, that sounds great," I replied.

We returned to the living room and resumed flipping through the albums. As we did, my eyes landed on a photo album titled "Our Wedding Day" on the shelf.

"Can I look through this one?" I asked, pointing to the album.

"Of course," Colleen said, handing it to me.

I opened the album and began to flip through the pages. The first few showed the beautiful scenery of the wedding, followed by pictures of the dress and the cake. The next few pages featured the bridesmaids, the groomsmen, and the flower girl. I smiled, enjoying the happy memories captured in the photos.

The next page showed white doves in cages.

"Oh that's interesting! You had doves at your wedding?" I asked.

"My husband insisted, he said how he couldn't have a wedding without one." Colleen said.

A flashback took over once again.

"What you doing mommy?" I asked my mom who was on the computer. She had a pen and a notebook with her, and she had her thinking glasses on meaning she was doing something really important.

"I'm trying to find these crazy birds your father wants for our Wedding renewal." she said.

"What's a wedding renewal?" I asked being the curious 5 year old.

"A wedding renewal is like when grown-ups have a special day to celebrate how much they love each other, just like they did when they first got married. It's kind of like a birthday party for their love, where they might dress up, say nice things to each other, and have fun with their friends and family all over again."

"Can I come to the wedding birthday party?" I asked eagerly.

Mom laughed, "Of course sweetie." She said kissing my cheek.

Dad walked in a few seconds later. "Daddy!" I yelled running up to him. "Hey bean!" He said picking me up. He gave me a kiss and then put me down. Walking over to mom, he kissed her forehead.

"Found the doves?" He asked.

"I don't think you know how hard it is to get doves last minute." She said giggling.

"Make it happen woman, I can't remarry the love of my life without the doves there to make it even more special." He said kissing her.

"Eww." I said covering my eyes.

The flashback vanished and I could just feel something wasn't sitting right.

I continued to look through the book, then I turned the page and froze. There, on the next page, was a picture of the bride and groom. The groom's face made my heart stop. I inched closer to see if what I was seeing was true.

"No, it can't be," I whispered, my hands shaking.

Carter noticed my sudden change in demeanor and leaned in to see what I was looking at.

"Caitlyn, what's wrong?" he asked, concerned.

I couldn't believe my eyes. I frantically flipped through more pages, looking at picture after picture. It was him. The groom was my father. The man who had left me and my mom when I was five was now part of Carter's family.

Just as the realization hit me, the front door opened. In walked the man himself – my dad. We both froze and stared at each other in shock.

"Dad?" I managed to whisper, my voice trembling.

# Chapter 20

I stood frozen, staring at the man in front of me. My mind raced as the realization hit me like a freight train.

His face went pale, his eyes widening in shock. "Caitlyn?" he whispered, taking a step towards me.

Without another word, I turned and bolted from the house, my heart pounding in my chest. I could hear Carter calling after me, but I didn't stop. I ran until I reached the park nearby, my breath coming in ragged gasps as I collapsed onto a bench, my mind spinning.

I felt the onset of a panic attack, my chest tightening as I struggled to breathe. Tears streamed down my face, and I wrapped my arms around myself, rocking back and forth in a desperate attempt to calm down.

"Caitlyn," a voice called out, and I looked up to see my father standing there, his face filled with concern.

"Stay away from me," I choked out, but he didn't listen. He approached me slowly, his hands raised in a placating gesture.

"Caitlyn, please," he said softly.

I shook my head, the tears blurring my vision. "No," I whispered, my voice trembling. "You don't get to be here now."

He knelt in front of me, his eyes filled with pain. "Look how beautiful you've become," he said, reaching out to touch my face.

I recoiled from his touch, shaking my head violently. "No," I cried. "You don't get to compliment me. You don't get to speak to me."

He pulled his hand back, his expression one of deep sorrow. "Caitlyn, please. I know I've made mistakes."

"Mistakes?" I echoed, my voice rising. "MISTAKES? You left me! You vanished without a word. You missed birthdays, graduations, every important moment in my life. Do you know what that did to me?" I yelled.

"Was I just a mistake to you, Dad?" I asked, my voice breaking.

His eyes filled with tears, but he said nothing, letting my words wash over him.

"Why?" I demanded, my voice cracking. "Why did you leave me? Why didn't you ever come back? Why didn't you try to get in touch with me? Do you have any idea how many nights I cried myself to sleep, wondering what I did wrong? Wondering how the hell I could have not been good enough for you at five fucking years old, Dad. FIVE! I was five, I didn't know a life without you, and yet you forced me to live one without you."

He bowed his head, the weight of my pain pressing down on him. "I'm so sorry, Caitlyn. I just... I had my reasons. In the end, I thought it would be best for you."

"Best for me?" I repeated, incredulous. "How could abandoning me be what's best for me? You left me with a mother who resents me, who's cold and distant. I don't even know who the fuck she is anymore. I needed you, Dad. I needed you to be there and you weren't."

He looked up at me, his eyes pleading. "I just thought you'd be better off without me Bean."

My anger flared, the years of pent-up hurt and betrayal spilling out. "Don't call me that! You don't get to decide that! You don't get to choose when to be a father and when to disappear. You promised you'd always be there for me, but you broke that promise. And now you have a new family, a new life, while I was left to pick up the pieces."

"I never stopped thinking about you," he said, his voice choked with emotion. "Not a day went by that I didn't regret leaving."

"Then why didn't you come back?" I cried, my voice raw. "Why didn't you fight for me? I needed you, Dad. I needed you to be there to teach me things, to protect me. I needed you to be my father."

"You don't know what I have been through that you could have helped me with. You don't know. You don't know. You just don't know." I cried.

"Caitlyn, I thought I was doing the right thing back then but I get it now."

I shook my head, the tears blurring my vision. "It's too late," I whispered. "You missed everything. You missed me growing up. You missed my life."

"I know," he said, his voice barely audible. "And I can never make that up to you. But I want to try, Caitlyn. Please, let me try."

I looked at him, my heart aching with a mixture of anger, sorrow, and the faintest glimmer of hope. "I don't know if I can ever forgive you," I said honestly. "But I do want answers. I want to understand why you thought leaving was the answer."

"And what? Did you know that Carter and I were dating? Did you just randomly decide you want a relationship with me now that you randomly seen me one day?" I asked.

"No, I promise I have been thinking about you non stop lately." He said.

"I'll answer any questions you have." He promised.

"Why couldn't you just tell me the truth?" I demanded. "Why did you leave me with so many questions? Why didn't you come back and face me?"

"Caitlyn," he said, his voice filled with anguish, "there's something you need to ask your mother. It's... it's complicated. But you need to hear it from her."

"Ask my mother?" I repeated, confused. "What do you mean? What is there left to say that she hasn't already told me?"

"Just... just ask her," he said, his voice tinged with regret. "There are things about my departure that I can't explain right now. But she can."

I stared at him, my heart aching with a mix of betrayal and sorrow. "You want me to just go to her and ask why you left? Why should I trust anything you say now? Why should I believe anything you tell me?"

"I know it's hard," he said, his voice breaking. "But I'm here now. I want to make things right. Please, give me a chance to explain. I'll do whatever it takes."

"I'm sorry," he said, his voice full of pain. "I'm so sorry, Caitlyn. I truly am."

I walked away from the park, my footsteps heavy and deliberate. As I approached my house, my phone was vibrating non-stop with calls from Carter. I couldn't bring myself to answer, not yet.

Just as I reached my front door, I heard a familiar voice behind me. "Caitlyn!" Carter called out, rushing to catch up.

I turned around, feeling the weight of the day pressing down on me. Carter was breathless, concern etched across his face. "Caitlyn, what's going on? Why did you run off like that?"

My frustration bubbled over. "I don't want to talk about it, Carter," I snapped, my voice colder than I intended.

"Caitlyn, you're scaring me. What happened?" he pressed, reaching out for my arm.

I jerked away from him. "It's not your business, Carter."

"But it is," he said, his voice tinged with desperation. "You just ran off. I need to know what's going on. Why were you so upset? Why did you call my stepdad 'Dad'?"

I took a deep breath, trying to keep my emotions in check. "Because that's my dad Carter."

Carter's eyes widened in shock. "What? Your father? But... but why—"

"Why?" I cut him off, my voice trembling with anger. "He thought he was doing what was best for me. But all he did was leave me with a mother who hates me. He missed my entire childhood and now he wants to waltz back into my life like nothing happened."

"I didn't know," Carter said quietly, his gaze dropping. "I had no idea he was your father."

"Exactly," I said sharply. "And you know what? I don't want to have anything to do with him. So you can go enjoy your life with him, if that's what you want. I'm done."

Carter looked pained, trying to understand. "Caitlyn, please. Just talk to him. You don't have to go through this alone. Let me help."

"Help?" I laughed bitterly. "How can you help? You don't even know the half of it. I'm not going to let him mess with my life anymore. I've had enough."

"Caitlyn, please," Carter begged, taking a step closer. "I know you're hurting, but shutting everyone out won't fix anything. You need to talk to him, figure things out."

I shook my head, tears mingling with the anger in my eyes. "I'm done talking. I'm done with him. I don't want to see him anymore."

"So what does this mean for us?" Carter asked, his face filled with gloom. I held in the tears. I couldn't date someone who is my fathers stepchild that's just weird and not right.

I stood there, struggling to find the right words. My heart was pounding, and I could feel the tears threatening to spill. "Carter, I... I don't know. This is just too much."

He looked at me, confusion and hurt mixing in his eyes. "What do you mean?"

"I mean... us," I said, my voice breaking. "I don't think we can do this."

Carter's face fell, his eyes wide with disbelief. "What? Caitlyn, why? We're... we're in this together remember. We can figure it out."

"I can't be with you, Carter. Not now, not like this. It's just too complicated," I said, tears welling up in my eyes. "My whole world is falling apart, and I need to deal with it on my own. I can't handle this... this connection to my dad, and the fact that you're his stepson. It's just too much."

Carter's eyes were filled with pain and confusion. "So you're just... ending things because of him? Because of this?"

"It's not just about him," I said, my voice cracking. "It's about everything that's happened. I need to focus on myself, on healing, and I can't do that while I'm trying to navigate this complicated mess with you. I'm sorry, Carter. I really am."

His shoulders slumped, and his voice was barely a whisper. "So that's it? You're just going to walk away?"

"I don't know what else to do," I admitted, my heart breaking as I spoke. "I'm too hurt and confused right now. I need space. I need to figure things out for myself."

Tears streamed down Carter's face as he tried to hold back his emotions. "Caitlyn, don't do this. We can work through it. I care about you. I want to be here for you."

"I know you do," I said, my own tears spilling over. "But right now, I can't. I need to be alone to process everything that's happened."

Carter took a deep breath, trying to compose himself and walked away. I watched as he walked away, his steps slow and heavy. I felt the weight of my decision and the pain of the situation pressing down on me. As he disappeared from view, I turned and walked back into my house, feeling the ache of my broken heart and the emptiness of the choices I had made.

# Chapter 21

I stumbled through the front door, my emotions still raw from the confrontation with my father. As soon as I walked in, my mother's harsh voice cut through the air.

"Where were you?" she spat, glaring at me from the kitchen. Her tone was icy, as if my mere presence was an inconvenience.

"Mom, don't start, please," I said, my voice tired and strained. I could barely muster the energy to deal with her right now.

"Don't start?" she echoed, her voice rising. "You think you can just come in here after disappearing all day and tell me what I can and can't do? Where were you, Caitlyn?"

"I was out," I snapped, trying to hold back my tears. "I needed to clear my head. After everything that's happened..."

"Oh, spare me the drama," she cut me off, her voice dripping with disdain. "What could you possibly need to clear your head from? You've got it so rough, don't you? With everything I've done for you."

I clenched my fists, trying to keep my composure. "Don't act like you care about me now, Mom. Not after everything you've done."

Her face twisted into a sneer. "Oh, and what exactly have I done? I've given you a roof over your head and food on the table. Isn't that enough?"

"That's not enough!" I shouted, my voice breaking. "It's never been enough! You think providing the basics is all it takes to be a mother? I needed you, Mom. I needed you to be there for me, not just physically, but emotionally."

She rolled her eyes, clearly uninterested in my outburst. "Look at you. You're just like your father—ungrateful and selfish."

"That's not fair!" I yelled, my anger boiling over. "Why are you always blaming me for everything? He's the one that left, but you still had me. Why wasn't I enough for you? Why couldn't you just be there for me? You shunned me as a daughter mom. I love you and I loved you even when you treated me like you didn't love me." I started to cry.

My mother's face hardened. "You know what? Maybe if you weren't so worthless, he wouldn't have left. He didn't want you. He never did."

Her words hit me like a punch to the gut. "What are you talking about?" I demanded, tears streaming down my face. "Why did he leave, really? What's the real reason?"

She let out a harsh laugh. "The real reason? He couldn't stand the thought of raising a child that wasn't his. You were a constant reminder of his failures. He didn't love you, Caitlyn. He never did."

I wasn't his?

"What do you mean a child that wasn't his?" I asked my voice trembling. "How could you just let him leave? How could you let him walk away from me like that?"

She sneered, her eyes cold and unforgiving. "He left because you weren't biologically his child."

I felt my legs give out beneath me, and I stumbled back against the wall, my heart pounding in my chest. "What are you talking about? You're telling me I was just a burden to him?"

She laughed bitterly, a sound that cut through me like a knife. "A burden? That's one way to put it. He never wanted you, Caitlyn. And when he found out he wasn't your biological father, it just made it easier for him to walk away."

I felt like the floor had dropped out from under me. "How could you do this to me? How could you let me grow up thinking he loved me? How could you stand there and watch me suffer, knowing the truth? Why couldn't you just tell me?"

Her face was a mask of hardened indifference. "Because I was too damn tired to deal with it. I was too busy trying to keep myself together while you whined about your pathetic life."

I choked on my anger, tears streaming down my face. "You think I wanted any of this? I didn't ask for this. I didn't ask for you to treat me like I was nothing. I was a child, Mom. I needed you, and all you did was push me away. And all you can say is that your roof and food were enough? They were never enough!"

She glared at me, her voice cold and sharp. "Maybe if you'd been a better daughter, things would have been different. But you were always so ungrateful, so demanding. Always bitching about God knows what. I did what I could, and it was never enough for you."

"Ungrateful?" I screamed, my voice cracking with emotion. "I was a kid! I tried to be the daughter you wanted, but nothing was ever good enough for *YOU*! And now you're telling me it's my fault? That I drove him away?"

"You were never good enough," she spat, her voice filled with bitterness. "You've always been a disappointment. I did what I had to do to survive, and if that meant pushing you away, then so be it."

Her words were like daggers piercing my heart, and I felt a surge of raw, uncontrollable fury. "You're a fucking monster, you know that? You should have been there for me. You should have fought for me. But instead, you forced me to deal with everything on my own!"

She flinched at my words, but the anger in her eyes didn't fade. "I did what I had to do to get by. Life is tough, Caitlyn. You should know that by now."

"I do know that!" I shouted, my voice echoing through the house. "But it's not just about surviving. It's about living, and you never gave me a chance to live. You were supposed to be my first best friend, my mother, but you left me with nothing but pain and abandonment!"

She looked at me, her eyes cold and distant. "He didn't love you Caitlyn, period. Get over it."

"What about you mom? Do you love me?" I asked my voice shaky. She just stared at me.

Her silence was all the answer that I needed. "And what about us?" I screamed, tears pouring down my face. "What about the fact that I needed you? I needed you to love me, to help me through this mess. But all I got was rejection and coldness!"

Her face twisted in a mix of anger and regret. "I'm not going to apologize for what I did. It's done. It's over. You want to blame me for everything? Fine. I can't change the past."

I felt like my heart was breaking into a thousand pieces. "I'm not just blaming you. I'm hurting. I'm devastated. And you're standing here, acting like none of it matters. Well, it does. It all matters. And I'm done with it. I'm done with you."

"You went out and had an affair and had me with someone else, didn't you?" I screamed, the accusation tearing from my throat like a wounded animal. "That's why he left. That's why he never wanted me. I was a mistake, a reminder of what YOU did wrong mom! Not me. This is YOUR problem."

My mother's face went pale, and for a moment, she looked as though she might collapse. "Caitlyn, I—"

"No," I interrupted, my voice filled with a fierce, desperate energy. "Don't try to justify it. Don't try to explain it away. You messed up my life. You ruined it. I was just a child, Mom, and you let me grow up thinking I was loved, only to find out I was never enough. You always said you were tired, that it was too hard. But you had a choice. You could have tried. You could have cared. But you didn't."

My mother's shoulders shook, and she looked at me with eyes that were now a mix of anger, guilt, and a profound weariness. "I was trying to survive, Caitlyn."

"You were supposed to survive WITH ME. Help me through! Instead, you just left me to fend for myself while you wallowed in your own misery."

She broke down then, her tears mixing with her anger. "I did the best I could with what I had. I wasn't perfect. I made mistakes. I was scared, and I didn't know how to fix things."

"Fix things?" I yelled, the pain and frustration spilling over. "You think you can just fix this? You can't fix it. You can't undo the years of hurt, the years of feeling worthless. You can't erase the damage you've done."

She sank into a chair, her head in her hands. "I didn't know how to be a mother. I thought if I just kept going, if I just kept working, everything would turn out okay."

"And look where that got us," I snapped. "I'm a mess. I don't even know myself. And you're standing here, making excuses."

"And I'm supposed to just forget all this?" I said, my voice cracking with emotion. "Forget how you abandoned me emotionally? Forget how you let me believe that I was never good enough? I can't just let it go. I can't just pretend it's all okay." Everything was starting to just spill it out now. All the years of pain and abuse.

"And then you go and you meet this dick of a guy, you bring him into our house, he takes over and tries to act like the man of the house. You have a baby with him and all you can see is how he provides financially. What you don't see, is that he doesn't take care of his child. Claire doesn't even know Steve. You don't see how he is abusive and mean, how he has sexually assaulted me multiple times mom! MULTIPLE TIMES. But everything I say is a fucking lie to you right? I haven't even told you about the times he'd come into my room when you were passed out drunk. How he would place his hand over my mouth and rape me.

You know why? Because you never believe a fucking word I say. I am done with you mom. I have lost all respect for you!" I screamed.

I staggered back, the raw pain of my words hanging heavy in the air. My mother's face drained of color, shock and denial flickering in her eyes.

"You once said to me that sometimes things aren't meant to be. Why couldn't you see that you and Steve were not meant to be mom?" I was angry.

"Caitlyn, what are you—"

"Don't," I cut her off, my voice steady despite the torrent of emotions raging within me. "Don't pretend you didn't know. I've tried to tell you, over and over. You chose to ignore me. You chose to believe that everything was fine as long as the bills were paid. I let you call me all kind of names, I let you use me as a punching bag all the time. I am done mom."

Her eyes widened, and for a moment, she looked lost. "I didn't know," she whispered, her voice trembling. "I didn't know it was that bad."

"Of course you didn't," I spat. "Because you never cared enough to see. You were too busy drowning in your own problems to notice mine. You think you were doing your best? Your best wasn't nearly enough."

"I'm sorry," she said, her voice trembling. "I didn't know how to handle it. I thought everything would be okay."

"Okay?" I demanded, my voice rising again. "You think this is okay? You think it's okay that I had to deal with all of this alone? That I had to endure Steve's abuse and your neglect while you drank away your problems?"

She shook her head, tears streaming down her face. "I didn't know," she repeated, her voice cracking. "I'm so sorry, Caitlyn. I never wanted any of this."

"Words don't fix years of pain and betrayal. You don't get to act like you were the victim here. You weren't. I was. And I'm done pretending that everything is okay."

"I know I've failed you," she said, her shoulders shaking with sobs. "I know I've made mistakes. I'm sorry for everything. I'm sorry for not protecting you."

"You've done too much damage mom."

Her face fell, and she looked away, her shoulders slumped in defeat. "I understand," she said quietly.

With that, I turned and walked away, leaving my mother standing alone in the kitchen. I quickly entered my room as I felt a wave of nausea hit me. I ran to the bathroom and threw up.

I sat on the bathroom floor, my body trembling with the aftermath of my emotional outburst, a chilling vision began to take hold. It started with the sound of my mother's voice, distorted and echoing through my mind. I could see her in the kitchen, her face a mask of despair. She was holding a bottle of pills, her hands shaking uncontrollably.

The scene played out with vivid clarity: my mother, her expression a mixture of resignation and sorrow, was pouring the pills into her palm. Her movements were slow, deliberate, as if each action was taken with immense effort. Her eyes, once cold and unfeeling, were now filled with a deep, hollow sadness.

She sat at the kitchen table, the pills before her, her fingers trembling as she picked up a glass of water. The vision was almost too painful to bear. I could feel the weight of her despair, her sense of hopelessness pressing down on me like a heavy blanket.

In a blur of emotion, I saw her drop the pills into her mouth, her face contorting with fear. She swallowed them with a gulp of water, her eyes closing as if bracing for what was to come.

The vision was so real, so intense, that I could almost hear the faint sound of the pills rattling against the glass. I felt a surge of panic, my heart racing as the realization of what I was witnessing sank in.

The vision ceased. I forced myself to stand, my legs weak and unsteady.

I stumbled back into the kitchen, my mind racing with a desperate need to stop her.

"Mom!" I shouted, my voice cracking with fear. I rushed to the kitchen, my eyes scanning for her.

I found her sitting at the table, the empty pill bottle beside her. She looked up at me, her eyes glazed over and distant. "Caitlyn..." she murmured, her voice barely audible.

I grabbed her by the shoulders, shaking her gently. "Mom, no! You can't do this! Please, just hold on!" I dialed 911 on my phone, calling the ambulance to come help my mother.

Her eyes met mine, and for a moment, I saw a flicker of the woman who had once been my mother, lost beneath the layers of pain and neglect.

"Caitlyn, I... I don't know how to fix things," she whispered, tears streaming down her face. "I've made so many mistakes."

"Forget about the mistakes," I said urgently. "Just stay with me. We'll figure this out. We have to."

Her shoulders trembled as she began to cry, and I wrapped my arms around her, trying to offer comfort despite the chaos of emotions swirling inside me.

"I'm so sorry, Caitlyn," she sobbed.

"Just don't give up," I pleaded, my voice breaking. "Please. We have to find a way through this. We can't let it end like this."

We stayed like that for what felt like an eternity, my mother clinging to me as if I were her lifeline. She looked up at me, tears streaming down her face and said,

"I want help."

# Chapter 22

It's been three weeks, and the events that has taken place has left me mentally and physically exhausted. Carter and I still haven't talked since that one night, I miss him, I will admit. I have been taking care of Claire, and Callie has helped me through majority of life's problems. My dad has tried to talk to me again, but I still can't muster the strength to even respond. Mom went under a 72 hour suicide watch hold, and she then was taken into a rehab facility. Today was the day I finally get to visit her and I was as nervous as ever.

The rehab center was quieter than I expected. The hum of air conditioning filled the space, and the faint scent of antiseptic lingered in the air. It was unsettling to see my mom here, in a place meant for people who needed help. But this is what she has needed all along.

I was ushered into a small, private room where she was waiting. When I saw her, she looked different—tired but somehow lighter, as if the weight of her demons was finally being addressed. She managed a weak smile when our eyes met.

"Hey, Mom," I said, taking a seat beside her. The awkwardness between us was thick, but there was a sliver of hope that hadn't been there before.

"Caitlyn," she murmured, her voice softer than I remembered. "I'm glad you came."

"How are you feeling?" I asked, unsure of how to navigate this new dynamic.

"Better," she admitted, looking down at her hands. "It's been... hard. But I'm trying."

I nodded, taking a deep breath. "That's good. I'm glad you're getting the help you need."

We sat in silence for a moment before I decided to ask the question that had been gnawing at me ever since I found out the truth. "Mom, I need to know something... I need you to tell me about my biological dad."

Her eyes flickered with something—regret, pain, maybe a mix of both. She hesitated, then finally nodded. "He was a sweet man, Caitlyn. We had a great relationship. I thought I loved him, but I was young and stupid. I made a mistake."

"What happened?" I pressed, leaning forward slightly.

She sighed, rubbing her temples as if the memory pained her. "I cheated on him. With your dad— your— you know. I don't know why I did it. Maybe I was trying to fill some void, something I couldn't even name back then. When he found out, it broke him. But he was still kind to me, kinder than I deserved. He wanted to work things out, but your dad found out about him through someone, a source I never figured out. And after that... everything just fell apart."

I absorbed her words, feeling a strange mix of sadness and anger. "So... you pushed him away."

She nodded, tears welling up in her eyes. "I didn't know how to keep him in my life after what I'd done. And then your dad stepped in. He made things... complicated. And I let him. I'm so sorry, Caitlyn. For everything I've put you through. I wish I could take it all back."

The rawness in her voice caught me off guard. It was the first time I'd ever seen her so vulnerable, so open. "I don't know if we can fix everything," I said slowly, "but maybe we can start over. Rebuild."

She nodded, wiping away a tear. "I'd like that."

We sat there for a while longer, just being in each other's presence. It wasn't perfect, but it was a beginning. And that was more than I had hoped for.

"How's my Claire?" She asked smiling a bit. "She's doing good." I smiled, thinking of my baby sister. "Your birthday's are coming up." She said and I nodded my head.

"If I'm out by then, maybe we can do something?" She asked as she gently took my hand. I let out a nervous breath. "I would love that mom." I said and I squeezed her hand against mine.

Later that afternoon, my phone buzzed with a message from Carter. He wanted to meet up, and I agreed. Again, we hadn't talked much since everything had come crashing down, and I wasn't sure how to approach the conversation we needed to have.

We met at the park, Carter was already there when I arrived, sitting on a bench, looking out at the pond.

"Hey," I greeted him as I sat down beside him.

"Hey," he replied, his voice heavy with something unspoken. "How's your mom?" I assumed Callie told him about everything that's happened with my mom.

"She's... doing better," I said. "She's getting the help she needs."

He nodded, his eyes still fixed on the water. "I'm glad to hear that."

There was a long pause before he finally spoke again. "I've been thinking a lot about what's happened. About my stepdad—about him being your dad. It's a lot to take in."

"I know," I said quietly. "It's been hard for me too. But I think... I think we need to face it, together."

Carter turned to look at me, his eyes searching mine. "How do we do that? How do we move forward with all this... history?"

The history was the least of my concerns, I needed to tell Carter about the visions. I longed for this day, I don't want him to think that I'm a psycho.

I took a deep breath. "There's something else I need to tell you. Something I've been keeping to myself because I didn't know how you'd react."

His brow furrowed with concern. "What is it?"

"I've been having visions," I confessed, my heart pounding in my chest. "They started a while ago, and they've been getting more intense. I see things—things that end up happening. Or things that has happened. It's hard to explain, but it's real."

For a moment, Carter just stared at me, processing what I'd said. Then, to my surprise, he reached out and took my hand. "Caitlyn, I don't understand everything that's happening, but I believe you. And I'm here for you."

Relief washed over me, and I squeezed his hand, grateful for his support. "Thank you, Carter. That means more to me than you know."

He smiled, a small, genuine smile that reminded me of better days. "So... does this mean we can try to make this work? Us, I mean?"

I hesitated, but only for a moment. "Yeah, I think we can."

As we sat there, hands entwined, I felt a sense of hope that maybe, just maybe, we could find a way to navigate the tangled mess our lives had become. It wouldn't be easy, but for the first time in a long time, I felt like it was possible.

# Chapter 23

The following day, I found myself standing outside Carter's house, my heart heavy with anticipation. I had spent the night tossing and turning, replaying the conversation with my mom in my head, and now, I was here, ready to face the man who had once been my dad—the man who had walked out of my life without explanation. Or at least that's what I use to think.

As I knocked on the door, a familiar anxiety gripped me. The door opened slowly, revealing my dad, who had once been my world. He looked older than I remembered, the years etched into his face, but his eyes held the same warmth I had clung to as a child.

"Caitlyn," he said softly, stepping aside to let me in. "I wasn't sure you'd come."

I walked into the house, the memories flooding back with every step. "I wasn't sure I'd come either," I admitted.

We settled in the living room, the silence between us thick and uncomfortable. Finally, he spoke. "I want you to know, Caitlyn, that leaving you was the hardest thing I've ever done. I thought I was doing the right thing, but I see now that I was wrong. I should have never left you, no matter the circumstance."

His words hit me like a wave, and I struggled to keep my emotions in check. "You left me," I said, my voice trembling. "All I knew was you. You were my dad, and then one day, you were just... gone."

He looked down, guilt evident on his face. "I know I hurt you, Caitlyn. I've spent every day regretting my decision. But I was scared. I was scared that I couldn't be the father you needed, especially with everything that was going on with your mom."

"That wasn't fair," I shot back, the anger I'd been holding onto for years bubbling to the surface. "It wasn't fair to me. I didn't care about any of that; I just wanted my dad."

He winced at my words, but I couldn't stop. "You were supposed to be the one person I could count on. How could you just walk away?"

Tears filled his eyes, and for the first time, I saw the pain he'd been carrying. "I'm so sorry, Caitlyn. I was a coward. I was angry at your mom and I took it out on you. She never told me you weren't mine, she made me think you were mine the whole time, and when I found out the truth, I just couldn't bare it."

The rawness in his voice matched the hurt in my heart. "I needed you though," I whispered, the tears finally spilling over. "I needed you, and you weren't there."

He reached out, but I pulled away, the distance between us now more than just physical. "I know I can't change the past," he said, his voice breaking. "But I want to try to make things right. I want to be in your life again, if you'll let me."

I stared at him, the man who had once been my hero, and felt the weight of everything that had happened between us. "It's not that easy," I said, my voice cracking. "You can't just come back and expect everything to be okay."

"I don't expect that," he said quickly. "I just want a chance to be the father you deserve. I know I've lost your trust, and I'll do whatever it takes to earn it back. I just... I just want to be there for you, Caitlyn."

His words hung in the air, and I didn't know what to say. A part of me wanted to forgive him, to let him back into my life, but another part of me was still that little girl who had cried herself to sleep, wondering why her dad had left her.

"I need time," I finally said, wiping away my tears.

He nodded, understanding in his eyes. "Take all the time you need. I'll be here, waiting. Just know that I love you, Caitlyn. I never stopped."

His words echoed in my heart as I stood up to leave. "I'll think about it," I said, my voice barely above a whisper. "But I can't make any promises."

I stood up, ready to leave, when the door creaked open, and Carter walked in. His eyes darted between me and his stepdad, sensing the tension in the room.

"Caitlyn," Carter greeted softly, coming over to stand beside me. He looked at his stepdad, then back at me, concern spread on his face. "I didn't mean to interrupt, but I wanted to be here with you."

His presence was comforting, grounding me in the moment. I nodded, grateful that he'd come.

My dad cleared his throat, clearly uneasy. "Carter, I wanted this to be a private talk."

"I wanted to be here for Caitlyn," Carter replied, his tone firm. "We've been through a lot together, and I care about her."

There was a pause, and I could see the gears turning in Carter's mind. He took a deep breath before asking the question that had likely been on his mind for a while. "How would you feel about us... being together? How would that work, given everything?"

My dad looked between us, his expression conflicted. "Carter, I—" he began, then hesitated, as if choosing his words carefully. "I care about you both. You've been like a son to me, and Caitlyn... well she's... she's my daughter."

He ran a hand through his hair, clearly grappling with his emotions. "It's complicated," he admitted. "But if you two care about each other and want to make it work, I won't stand in your way. I just want what's best for both of you."

I felt a strange sense of relief at his words, but there was still a lingering uncertainty. "But how would that even work?" I asked, voicing the concern that had been gnawing at me. "You're his stepdad, and you were like a dad to me... How do we navigate that?"

My dad sighed, looking weary. "I won't pretend it's easy. But relationships are complicated, and they don't always fit into neat little boxes. What matters is how you two feel and how you handle it. If you both decide this is what you want, then you'll find a way to make it work."

Carter reached for my hand, his grip reassuring. "We'll figure it out, Caitlyn."

I looked at Carter, then at the man who had been my father in all the ways that counted, even if not by blood. There was still a lot to work through, a lot of pain and confusion to untangle, but maybe, just maybe, there was a way forward.

"Okay," I said softly, squeezing Carter's hand. "We'll try."

My dad nodded, a flicker of something like hope in his eyes. "I'm glad to hear that. And Caitlyn... I meant what I said earlier. I want to be in your life, if you'll let me."

I took a deep breath, feeling the weight of the decision before me. "I need time," I repeated, but this time, there was a note of possibility in my voice.

He smiled faintly. "I understand."

As Carter and I left the house together, I felt a sense of closure I hadn't expected. There were still questions, still challenges ahead, but for the first time, I felt like maybe, just maybe, we could navigate them together.

# Chapter 24

At lunch, I found myself sandwiched between Carter and Callie, the three of us perched on the edge of a low wall near the school cafeteria. The sun was out, and I could almost pretend everything was normal. But with everything that had happened, normal felt like a distant memory.

Callie was animated, her hands waving around as she recounted a story about one of her classes. "And then, Mr. Hopkins just stared at him like he couldn't believe it. I swear, the guy's face turned every shade of red."

Carter chuckled beside me, but I couldn't shake the feeling that we were all just going through the motions. It wasn't until I spotted a familiar face walking toward us that I sat up straighter, my heart skipping a beat.

"Josh!" I called out, waving him over.

He grinned when he saw me, his steps quickening. "Hey, Caitlyn, Carter, Callie," he greeted, his tone light, but there was something different about him—a kind of relief that hadn't been there before.

"You're back," I said, smiling up at him. Josh had been gone for a few days, I was worried because I haven't heard much about him. "How are you?"

Josh nodded, his smile widening. "Yeah, I'm back. And things are... better. A lot better, actually. My mom and I moved in with my grandma, so, you know, no more... problems." His eyes met mine, and I could see the gratitude there. He didn't need to say more; I knew what he meant.

"That's amazing," I said softly, reaching out to give his arm a gentle squeeze. "I'm really glad, Josh. You deserve this."

"Thanks," he said, his voice thick with emotion. "It's still weird, adjusting, but it's a good weird, you know?"

Carter clapped him on the back. "You've been through a lot, man. It's good to see things turning around for you."

"Yeah, definitely," Callie chimed in, her usual sass taking a backseat to genuine kindness. "You deserve a break, Josh."

As we chatted, I felt a sense of warmth, like we were all starting to come together again after everything that had happened. But then, out of the corner of my eye, I saw Mike saunter into the cafeteria, a girl hanging onto his arm.

Callie noticed him too, her eyes narrowing slightly. I hesitated before asking, "Callie, how do you feel about that?"

She followed my gaze and snorted. "You mean Mike and his new shadow? Please, Caitlyn, I don't care. Besides, look at her." She gestured dismissively. "She's not even cute. I mean, I'm not exactly losing sleep over that downgrade."

I bit back a smile. Callie had a way of making everything seem so much smaller, less important. "You're right," I agreed, nudging her. "Definitely a downgrade."

Carter, who had been watching the exchange, shook his head with a small laugh. "You two are something else."

Callie flashed him a grin. "Hey, if you've got it, flaunt it. And if you don't... well, good luck to you."

Josh chuckled, relaxing even more into the easy banter. "I missed this," he admitted, his voice softer. "It's nice to be back."

"Yeah nice to not have an asshole picking on people everyday." Callie added hinting to Josh.

"Hey, people change." He said.

"Thank God." Carter, Callie and I said simultaneously as we all laughed.

After school, Claire and I settled in front of the TV, the familiar jingle of *The Talking Eraser Show* filling the living room. Claire was curled up next to me, giggling at the silly antics on the screen, but my mind was elsewhere.

Suddenly, there was a knock at the door. I frowned, glancing at the clock. It was late, and we weren't expecting anyone. Claire looked up at me, her eyes wide with curiosity.

"Stay here," I told her, getting up and walking toward the door. I peeked through the window, my breath catching when I saw who it was. The old woman.

I opened the door slowly, a mix of surprise and curiosity bubbling inside me. "Hi," I greeted, stepping aside to let her in. "I wasn't expecting you."

She smiled, a warm, almost knowing smile that made the hairs on the back of my neck stand up. "I thought it was time we talked, officially." she said, her voice soft but firm.

I led her into the living room, where Claire was still engrossed in the show. "Claire, why don't you go upstairs and finish watching in your room?" I suggested gently. Claire pouted but obeyed, giving the old woman a curious glance before heading up the stairs.

Once we were alone, I turned to the old woman, the questions I'd been holding back rushing to the surface. "Are you... dead?" I asked bluntly, unable to hold it in any longer. "I mean, why don't you talk much? Am I just seeing a ghost?"

To my surprise, she laughed—a soft, melodic sound that filled the room. "No, Caitlyn, I'm very much alive," she assured me. "People in this town love their rumors. I just keep to myself, and that's all it takes for stories to start."

I exhaled, a weight lifting off my chest. "So, you're real," I murmured, more to myself than to her.

"Yes, I'm real," she confirmed, her eyes twinkling with amusement.

"Why did you always stare at me so creepily?" I said. "You never really talked, and it was... weird."

"I suppose I must have seemed strange to you," she admitted, her eyes twinkling. "I wasn't trying to be creepy, Caitlyn. I was just... watching over you, in a way. I didn't want to interfere before you were ready."

"Ready for what?" I asked, still feeling a bit unsettled by the whole thing.

"Ready to understand," she said simply. "You were always meant to know these things, but timing is important. I needed to make sure you were prepared."

I hesitated, the memory of that day at the grocery store flashing in my mind. "And what about Claire? That day at the store, you were holding her hand. Why did you do that?"

Her expression softened. "That day, Claire was wandering off, and I was concerned she might get lost. I didn't want to frighten her, so I held her hand to keep her safe until you noticed. I didn't mean to alarm you."

I nodded slowly, the explanation making sense but still leaving me with more questions. "And I'm here because there's more you need to see." She said.

Before I could ask what she meant, the familiar sensation of being pulled into a vision took over. The living room faded away, replaced by the scene of a woman—much younger than the old woman—lying in a hospital bed, cradling a newborn baby boy.

"What's his name?" The doctor asked.

The woman smiled as she stared at her baby.

"Christian" She stated.

The name "Christian" echoed in my mind as the vision unfolded, showing Christian growing up, living a full and happy life.

I watched as Christian went to school, graduated. I watched him go off to college where he met a special girl. The vision showed years going by, he ended up marrying the woman.

"To Christian and Kiya." The minister made a toast.

My heart skipped a beat as I recognized her—the same Kiya I had helped get to the hospital from the park. The vision continued, showing the tragic accident that claimed Christian's life, and suddenly, everything clicked into place. The very first vision I'd ever had—the car accident— the guy who's tire popped off, was of Christian.

The vision ended abruptly, leaving me gasping for breath. I blinked, trying to process what I had just seen. "So... the Kiya vision and the Christian vision... they're connected," I said slowly, the realization settling in.

The old woman nodded, her expression solemn. "Yes, Caitlyn. Christian was my son."

I stared at her, the pieces of the puzzle falling into place. "So that's why I've been seeing all of this," I whispered. "It's all connected to you."

She reached out, placing a gentle hand on my arm. "There's still more you need to understand, Caitlyn. But for now, just know that you are part of this, too."

I swallowed hard, my mind racing with questions. "Will you tell me more?"

She smiled again, that same knowing smile. "I will. But for now, rest. I'll come back when the time is right."

With that, she stood and left, leaving me standing in the middle of the living room, my mind spinning with everything I had just learned. There was so much more to this story—so much more I needed to understand. But for now, all I could do was wait.

# Chapter 25

The school day felt like a blur. My mind was a whirl of visions from the old woman's visit, and I knew I needed to share everything with Callie and Carter.

As the first bell rang, signaling the beginning of classes, I spotted Callie and Carter waiting by their lockers, chatting about the latest school drama. I took a deep breath and walked over to them, my heart pounding in my chest.

"Hey, can we talk for a minute?" I asked, trying to keep my voice steady. "There's something important I need to tell you."

Callie raised an eyebrow, her curiosity piqued. "Important? What's up?"

Carter's face mirrored Callie's concern. "Yeah, what's going on babe?"

I hesitated for a moment, struggling to find the right words. "It's about the old woman. She came by my house last night."

Callie's eyes widened. "She did? What did she want?"

I took a deep breath, choosing my words carefully. "She's not dead. That's just a rumor. She actually came to talk to me about the visions I've been having."

Carter frowned. "Visions? You mean the ones you've mentioned before?"

I never really told Carter about the old woman, until now.

I nodded. "Yes. She told me that almost everything I've seen is connected to her and her family. She showed me some new visions last night."

Callie leaned in, intrigued. "New visions? What did you see?"

"The most important thing," I said, trying to steady my voice, "was about her son. His name is Christian."

Carter's eyebrows shot up. "Christian? That name sounds familiar. What's the connection?"

I felt a lump in my throat. "Christian was part of my very first vision— the car accident. I saw his entire life. He grew up, went to school, got married... to a woman named Kiya."

Callie's eyes widened. "Kiya? The same one you helped get to the hospital?"

I nodded, feeling a knot of tension in my chest. "Yes, that's right. The old woman showed me how Christian and Kiya's lives were intertwined with my visions. Christian's life, his death—it all connects to what I've been seeing."

Carter looked at me, his expression a mix of concern and curiosity. "So, what does this mean for you? And for us?"

"It means," I said, trying to keep my voice calm, "that there's a lot more to this than I initially realized. The old woman is connected to all of it, and she's a part of my story too. But I don't fully understand everything yet."

Callie's expression softened. "That's a lot to take in. We are here with you."

Carter nodded in agreement. "Absolutely. If you need to talk or need help figuring things out, we've got your back."

I felt a surge of gratitude. "Thank you. I'm still trying to make sense of everything, but knowing you're here helps."

As we headed to lunch, Callie and Carter chatted about their weekend plans, but my mind was still grappling with the revelations.

During lunch, I tried to focus on their conversation, though my thoughts kept drifting back to the visions and the old woman's messages. Callie noticed my distraction and nudged me.

"Hey, you've been awfully quiet today," she said, her voice laced with concern. "Everything okay?"

I forced a smile. "Yeah, just thinking about everything. It's a lot to process."

Carter gave me a reassuring look. "I understand."

The rest of lunch passed in a haze. After the final bell rang, I excused myself from Callie and Carter, claiming I needed to go to the bathroom. My thoughts were racing as I walked down the hall, my mind still reeling from the morning's revelations. I needed to be alone for a moment to collect my thoughts.

Once inside the bathroom, I took a deep breath and leaned against the sink. The cool tile felt soothing under my hands as I closed my eyes, trying to steady my breathing. Suddenly, the sensation of being pulled into a vision swept over me.

The bathroom faded away, replaced by a cozy living room from what looked like decades ago. I saw a young woman sitting on a couch, her face illuminated by the soft light of a lamp. She was laughing and talking with a young man who had an easygoing charm about him. The voices seemed oddly familiar. It took a moment, but the realization hit me: this was Christian.

I watched as the young woman and Christian exchanged smiles and gestures of affection. It was clear they were in the early stages of their relationship, their eyes full of promise and dreams. They seemed so happy, so full of life.

Then, Christian stood up and walked over to a side table, picking up a photograph. The woman turned to look at him, and as she did, I saw her face clearly for the first time. It wasn't Kiya. My breath caught in my throat as recognition hit me like a bolt of lightning. It was my mother.

The vision abruptly ended, and I was back in the bathroom, my heart racing. I stared at my reflection in the mirror, trying to process what I had just seen. The implications were overwhelming. If my mom had been with Christian back then, did that mean Christian was my biological father?

Panic and excitement mingled in my chest as I realized I needed to find the old woman immediately. The pieces of the puzzle were starting to fall into place, but I needed more answers.

I dashed out of the bathroom and out of the school, my mind focused on finding the old woman. My heart pounded as I sprinted down the sidewalk, hoping she was still in town. The urgency of the moment drove me forward, my thoughts racing as I searched for the answers I so desperately needed.

# Chapter 26

My breath came in short, hurried gasps as I raced down the familiar streets. The vision I'd just witnessed was too intense, too real, to ignore. I needed answers, and I knew exactly where to find them.

I rushed through the park, my thoughts tangled with the intensity of the vision I'd just experienced. The sun was dipping low in the sky but I barely noticed. My mind was fixated on one thing: finding the old woman.

The park was almost empty, the usual crowd thinning out as evening approached. I headed towards a secluded area where the trees grew dense and the sounds of the city faded into the background. It was a place where I could think, and more importantly, a place where I knew I could find her.

Sure enough, as I approached a small clearing surrounded by towering oaks, there she was. The old woman stood with her back to me, her long, silver hair flowing gently in the breeze. She didn't turn around, but I knew she was aware of my presence.

"I saw something," I said breathlessly, coming to a stop a few feet away from her. "In the bathroom at school. It was a vision of Christian and a woman... my mom."

She turned slowly to face me, her eyes soft with understanding. "I've been waiting for this moment, Caitlyn."

I swallowed hard, trying to steady myself. "Is it true? Is Christian my father?"

She nodded, her expression gentle. "Yes, Christian was your father. And I am your grandmother, Elanor."

The weight of her words hit me like a tidal wave, nearly knocking the wind out of me. I stared at her, trying to process what she had just said. My grandmother? Christian was my father? It felt like the ground was shifting beneath me.

"I had a feeling, but hearing it..." My voice trailed off as I struggled to find the right words.

The old woman motioned for me to sit on a nearby bench. I obeyed. She sat beside me, her gaze never leaving mine.

"There's so much you don't know," she began, her voice soft yet steady. "Our family has a legacy, they've been passed down through generations, from my grandmother, to my mother, to Christian... and now, to you. The visions you've been having—they're part of that legacy."

I looked down at the golden locket around my neck, the one she had given me. "This locket... it's connected to the visions, isn't it?"

She nodded again. "Yes. The locket is a symbol of the gift that runs in our family."

I squeezed her hand, feeling a surge of emotion. "What happens now? What am I supposed to do?"

"You learn to embrace your gift," she said, her voice steady and full of warmth. "The visions are a part of you, and they can guide you if you learn to trust them. They connect you to the past, present, and future, and through them, you can help others."

I felt a wave of anxiety wash over me. "But what if I can't handle it? What if the visions get worse?"

She smiled gently, her eyes filled with wisdom. "The visions will become more frequent now that you know the truth, but they don't have to control you. And I'm here to help you, every step of the way."

Tears finally spilled over as I looked at her, feeling an overwhelming sense of gratitude and relief. "Thank you," I whispered, my voice shaking with emotion.

She pulled me into a hug, holding me close. "You're not alone, Caitlyn. You never have been. Together, we'll work through this."

Elanor took a deep breath, her gaze distant as she began. "The first time I had a vision, I was around 7. It was terrifying because I didn't know what was happening. I was in my bedroom, and suddenly I was somewhere else, seeing things that didn't make any sense. I thought I was losing my mind."

I leaned in closer, hanging on her every word. "What did you see?"

She smiled faintly. "It was a vision of my own mother, back when she was young. I saw her in a time before I was born, living a life I'd never known about. It was so vivid, so real, that when I snapped back to my own time, I was shaken to my core. I didn't understand what I'd seen or why."

"How did you figure it out?" I asked, my voice barely above a whisper.

"It took time," she admitted, "and a lot of fear and confusion. But eventually, my own mother sat me down and explained that our family has a gift, a gift that has been passed down through generations. She told me that her mother had it too, and that it was something that connected us to our ancestors and to those who would come after us. The visions were a way to understand the past and guide the future."

I nodded slowly, the pieces of the puzzle starting to come together. "So you learned to control them?"

Elanor smiled warmly. "In a way. It's not so much about control as it is about acceptance. The more I accepted the visions as a part of who I was, the easier it became to navigate them. I learned to trust them, to let them guide me rather than frighten me."

I looked down at my hands, thinking about all the visions I'd had and how they'd shaped my life without me even realizing it. "But why me? Why now?"

"Because you're ready," Elanor said simply. "You've grown strong enough to handle the truth, to carry the legacy forward. Again the visions will come more frequently now, but they will also give you the power to help others, to make a difference in ways you might not even imagine yet."

I took a deep breath, trying to let her words sink in.

"You continue to live your life, but with an open heart and mind," she advised. "Trust in the visions, and trust in yourself."

The weight of her words settled over me like a warm blanket, comforting and reassuring. I knew this wouldn't be easy, but I also knew that I had a guide, someone who understood what I was going through.

"Thank you, Elanor," I said softly. "I don't know how I would've gotten through this without you."

She reached out and gently touched the locket around my neck. "You're stronger than you realize, Caitlyn. This locket has been worn by generations of women in our family, each of them strong in their own way. And now it's your turn to carry it forward."

I squeezed her hand, feeling a new sense of resolve. Whatever was coming, I would face it head-on, with the strength of those who came before me and the guidance of my grandmother by my side.

"Can you help me with one thing?" I asked. Elanor looked at me and raised an eyebrow.

"Sure, what is it?"

# Chapter 27

Elanor's hand was warm and steady as she led me through the quiet streets toward Kiya's house. My mind raced with anticipation and nerves, the reality of what was about to happen settling heavily in my chest. I was about to see Kiya again and my half-brother and reveal a truth that would change everything.

As we approached Kiya's home, my heart pounded in my chest. What if she didn't accept me? What if this truth was too much for her to handle? Elanor squeezed my hand, sensing my unease, and gave me a reassuring smile.

"You're not alone in this, Caitlyn," she said softly. "Kiya is a good person. She'll understand."

I nodded, trying to steady my breathing as Elanor knocked on the door. Moments later, it opened to reveal Kiya, her eyes lighting up in surprise and warmth when she saw us.

"Elanor," she greeted, her voice full of genuine happiness. "What brings you here?"

"Oh my gosh Caitlyn?" Kiya asked clearly recognizing and remembering who I was.

"Hi again." I said shyly.

Kiya embraced me into a hug. "Oh my goodness, hi! I have been thinking of you so much." She stated.

"Same here." I smiled, the nerves in my body still jumping.

"We need to talk, Kiya," Elanor began gently. "There's something important you need to know."

Kiya's smile faltered slightly, a look of concern crossing her face, but she stepped aside and welcomed us in. I followed Elanor inside, my stomach churning with a mix of excitement and fear.

We sat down in her cozy living room, the baby monitor softly humming in the background. I could hear faint cooing noises from baby Christian, and my heart jumped at the thought of him being my brother.

Elanor took a deep breath, her expression serious yet calm. "Kiya, what I'm about to tell you might come as a shock, but it's important that you hear it."

Kiya nodded, her eyes flicking between Elanor and me.

"Caitlyn," Elanor began, "is Christian's biological daughter. That makes her your son's half-sister."

Kiya's eyes widened in disbelief, her mouth opening slightly as she processed the words. She looked at me, her gaze searching for confirmation, and I nodded, feeling a lump form in my throat.

For a moment, the room was silent, the weight of the revelation hanging heavy in the air. Then, Kiya's expression softened, tears welling up in her eyes as she reached out to me.

"Oh, Caitlyn," she whispered, her voice thick with emotion. "I had no idea..."

The tears that had been threatening to spill over finally did, and I couldn't hold back any longer. I threw my arms around her, feeling a rush of relief as she hugged me tightly in return.

"You're his daughter," Kiya murmured, pulling back slightly to look into my eyes. "That means so much... you have no idea how much that means to me."

"I didn't know," I said, my voice trembling. "I didn't know until recently. But I'm so glad... I'm so glad to know now."

Kiya wiped away her tears, a soft smile breaking through. "You're amazing, Caitlyn. I never forgot how you helped me that day at the park. I always felt there was something special about you, and now I know why."

Her words wrapped around me like a warm embrace, and I felt a deep connection forming between us—a bond that went beyond blood.

"And Christian," she continued, her voice gentle as she spoke of her son, "He's your brother. He's a part of you, just like you're a part of him."

I nodded, my heart swelling with emotion. "I want to be a part of his life, Kiya. I want to be there for him, for both of you."

Kiya's smile grew, and she took my hand, squeezing it tightly. "We're a family now, Caitlyn. You always have a place with us."

Elanor watched us with a proud, loving expression, and I could see the weight lifting from her shoulders. The truth was out, and instead of tearing us apart, it had brought us closer together.

As we sat together, the baby monitor suddenly crackled to life with a soft cry. Kiya smiled, excusing herself to check on Christian, leaving me and Elanor alone for a moment.

"You did well, Caitlyn," Elanor said, her voice full of warmth. "This is just the beginning. There's so much more ahead, but I know you're ready for it."

I smiled through my tears, feeling a sense of peace I hadn't felt in a long time. "Thank you, Elanor. For everything."

She reached over and touched the locket around my neck, her eyes shining with pride. "You're carrying on a legacy, Caitlyn, and I couldn't be more proud of you."

Kiya returned with Christian in her arms, his tiny face peeking out from beneath a blanket. She handed him to me, and as I held my brother for the first time, I felt a wave of love so powerful it took my breath away.

"Welcome to the family," Kiya said softly, her eyes full of warmth.

And in that moment, I knew that no matter what visions came my way, no matter how daunting the future seemed, I would face it all with the strength and love of the family I had found.

# Chapter 28

I walked into the rehab facility. It was strange being here again, seeing the place where my mom had been working to pull her life together. I tried to steady my nerves as I approached the room where my mom was staying.

When I pushed the door open, I found her sitting by the window, gazing out at the garden below. She looks better every time. But when she turned to face me, the weariness in her eyes was still there, a reminder of the struggles she was fighting to overcome.

"Hey, Mom," I said softly, stepping into the room.

"Caitlyn," she replied, her voice filled with a mix of surprise and relief. "Hi baby, it's good to see you."

I sat down across from her, trying to find the right way to start. There was so much to say, and I didn't know where to begin. But I knew I had to tell her everything.

"Mom," I began, my voice trembling slightly, "there's something I need to tell you. Actually, a lot of things."

She looked at me with concern, her eyes searching mine. "What is it, Caitlyn?"

I hesitated for a moment, then dove in. "I've been having visions. They started a while ago, but recently, they've become more frequent and intense."

Her eyes widened, and she leaned back in her chair. "Visions?" she echoed, almost as if confirming what she had just heard. "Just like your father."

Her words hit me like a punch to the gut. I knew she was referring to Christian. The fact that she knew this, that she was already connecting the dots, made this conversation both easier and harder.

"Yeah," I said softly, nodding. "Just like him."

She sighed, her eyes filling with a mix of sadness and understanding. "I always wondered if you'd inherit that from him. It's something that ran deep in his family."

I swallowed hard, feeling the weight of her words. "I met his mother. She... she told me everything, Mom. About Christian, about his visions, about our family's legacy."

Mom's face paled, and she clasped her hands together tightly. "You met Elanor?"

I nodded. "She's been helping me understand everything. She told me about Christian's death... how he died in a car accident." My voice cracked, and I could see the pain in my mom's eyes as I continued. "It was one of the first visions I ever had, but I didn't realize what it was until she explained it to me."

Tears welled up in my mom's eyes, and she looked away, blinking rapidly.

"I didn't know that he passed." She said holding in her tears.

I nodded my head sympathetically. "He did, I'm sorry." I said. My mom took a deep breath as she tried to process what I just told her.

"I never wanted you to find out like this," she whispered. "I tried to protect you from all of it."

"I know, Mom," I said, reaching out to take her hand. "But I needed to know the truth."

She squeezed my hand tightly, her own trembling. "Christian... he was so special."

"There's more," I said, steeling myself for what was to come. "Christian had a son... a baby boy. He's my half-brother."

Mom's eyes widened even further, shock and confusion flickering across her face. "A son? I didn't know... I had no idea."

I nodded. "His name is Christian too. He's just a baby, but... it's like this whole other part of my life I never knew existed."

Mom stared at me, her expression a mix of disbelief and sorrow. "I wish I could have told you everything, Caitlyn. I just didn't know how."

I shook my head. "It's okay, Mom. I'm finding out now, and that's what matters."

There was one more thing, the biggest revelation yet. I took a deep breath, bracing myself. "Mom... I'm back in contact with Dad."

Her entire body froze, and she looked at me, wide-eyed and speechless. "What? How... where is he?"

My heart pounded in my chest as I explained. "I'm dating Carter, and his stepdad... his stepdad is dad."

She gasped, her hand flying to her mouth. "No... no, that can't be."

"It's true," I said softly. "He told me he left because he knew I wasn't his biological daughter, and he couldn't handle it. But now... now we're trying to figure things out."

Mom was visibly shaken, her eyes brimming with tears. "I never wanted this for you, Caitlyn. I never wanted you to go through what I did."

"I know, Mom," I said, my voice breaking. "But I'm handling it. I have to."

She reached out, pulling me into a tight embrace, her tears mingling with mine. "I'm so sorry," she whispered, her voice choked with emotion. "I'm so sorry for everything."

I held her close, feeling the weight of all the pain, and all the love we still had for each other. "It's okay, Mom. We'll get through this. Together."

She nodded against my shoulder, her sobs quieting as we held onto each other. "Thank you for telling me," she murmured. "Thank you for trusting me with this."

"I had to," I said, pulling back to look at her. "You're my mom, and I needed you to know."

Her eyes, still red from crying, held a newfound determination. "I'm going to get better, Caitlyn. For you, for Claire... for all of us."

I nodded, feeling a sense of hope amidst all the chaos. "We'll get through this, Mom. One step at a time."

# Chapter 29

I walked into the cozy, dimly lit restaurant with Claire at my side. She held my hand tightly, her small fingers warm against my own. As we settled into our table, my dad arrived. The sight of him brought a flood of mixed emotions—nostalgia, apprehension, and hope.

"Hi, Dad," I greeted him with a nervous smile.

"Hey, Caitlyn," he replied, his voice holding a hint of uncertainty. He bent down to greet Claire, who looked up at him with curious eyes. "And who's this?"

"This is Claire," I said, guiding her closer. "Claire, this is my... dad." Claire gave him a shy smile. "Hi."

"Hi there, Claire," he said softly. "Nice to meet you."

We sat down, and the conversation soon turned to more personal matters. My dad's concern was evident as he asked, "How's your mom doing?"

I took a deep breath, feeling a mix of relief and sadness. "She's doing a lot better. She's in rehab now, working hard to get the help she needs. It's been a long road, but she's making progress."

"I'm glad to hear that," he said, nodding with genuine concern. "It's good she's getting the help she needs."

"So what are you having?" My dad asked as we scanned through the menu.

"I'm thinking the pasta." I smiled. "Great choice, how about you Claire?" He asked Claire who was coloring her menu with crayons. She looked up once she heard her name.

"Uh nuggies." she said and my dad and I laughed.

Dinner passed with comfort. We talked about the past, the present, and tried to navigate the gaps that had formed over the years. By the end of the meal, I felt a sense of closure, a small but significant step in reconnecting with a part of my past.

After we said our goodbyes and headed home, Carter and Callie arrived. Claire was on the couch, completely absorbed in "The Talking Eraser Show." The colorful characters on the screen had her full attention.

Callie glanced at the TV and smirked. "Seriously, we have to watch erasers?"

I laughed, feeling some of the day's tension lift. "Yep, Claire's obsessed with them. It's her favorite show right now."

Carter and Callie settled into the living room. I took a deep breath, ready to share the latest chapter of my story. "I have something important to tell you both," I began, looking at them.

Callie and Carter turned their full attention to me, sensing the gravity of my tone. "What's up?" Callie asked, her eyes wide with curiosity.

I glanced at Claire to make sure she was still engrossed in her show before continuing. "I met up with Elanor again—she's my grandmother."

Carter's eyebrows shot up in surprise. "Elanor? The old woman?"

"Like the creepy bitch?" Callie asked and I let out a small laugh.

I nodded. "Yes. Elanor is Christian's mother. Christian... he's my biological father."

Callie's eyes widened in disbelief. "Wait, Christian? The guy from the visions? Like Kiya's Christian?"

"Exactly," I said. "Elanor's been helping me understand everything. She's the one who gave me the locket and explained the family legacy of visions."

Carter's face softened with understanding. "Wow, Caitlyn. That's a lot to process."

Callie looked between us, trying to absorb the information. "So, Elanor is really your grandma? And Christian was your dad?"

I nodded. "Yes. It's been overwhelming, but it's also given me a lot of clarity about the visions and my family."

"And kiya? She had baby christian and that makes him my.. you know.. half brother." I added.

Callie's expression shifted from shock to admiration. "That's incredible. I mean, I can't believe how much you've been through and how it all connects. Elanor must be amazing to help you through this."

"She is," I said, feeling a sense of gratitude for the support. "She's been guiding me and helping me understand how to use the visions."

Carter reached out and squeezed my hand. "I'm really glad you have her. And I'm glad you're sharing all this with us. It must be a lot to handle."

Callie nodded in agreement, her eyes filled with empathy. "Yeah, Caitlyn. You're really brave for facing all this."

Callie's eyes lit up. "Wow, this is incredible! So you have a psychic grandma now?"

I chuckled, feeling the tension ease. "Yeah, she's been amazing, once she.. you know stopped being creepy."

Callie, always ready to lighten the mood, added, "Well, I guess we'll all have to get used to having a psychic around. Can you predict when the erasers are going to be done?"

I laughed, enjoying the warmth of their support and humor. The room was filled with laughter and light-hearted banter.

Eventually, Carter turned to me with a thoughtful expression. "So, what are you planning for your birthday? It's coming up soon, right?"

I glanced at Claire, still engrossed in her show, and then back at Carter and Callie. "Honestly, I just want to make sure Claire has an awesome day. We share a birthday, and she's been through a lot. I want her to have something special."

As I spoke, Claire remained absorbed in the erasers' antics, her giggles punctuating the air. She didn't hear our conversation, but I felt content knowing that focusing on Claire's happiness was the most important thing right now.

Carter and Callie smiled warmly, and the evening continued with easy conversation and laughter.

"Do you have any Twinkies?" Callie asked randomly.

I giggled, "Unfortunately I do not." I said.

Callie pretended to faint.

"The betrayal is real, you know I can't function without my Twinkies." She said as she groaned.

Claire started to laugh loud as she continued to watch the erasers on the TV screen. I looked at Callie as she gave me the straightest face.

"Yeah no, I'm going to go to my house and grab a box, there is no way I can get through this without them." Callie said getting up and walking out. Carter and I laughed hysterically.

"I am so proud of you." Carter said as he grabbed my hands and stared into my eyes.

"You have been through so much, and look at you. A queen. My queen." He stated and I blushed.

"Thank you Carter, you have made this journey less difficult." I said as I leaned in to kiss him.

Our lips met and we pulled away and stared at each other more.

"Eww" Claire yelled.

Carter and I laughed.

"What?" I asked Claire.

"Boys are stinky remember." She said and we both laughed hysterically again.

# Chapter 30

Two weeks had passed and today marked a bittersweet milestone: Claire and I were celebrating our birthdays. It was a clear, crisp morning, and I was determined to make it special for Claire. We had breakfast plans at her favorite breakfast place, a small, cheerful place with colorful murals and a menu full of pancakes, waffles, and other kid-friendly delights.

As we arrived at the diner, Claire bounced excitedly in her seat, her eyes wide with anticipation. She clutched her stuffed bunny tightly, its floppy ears flapping as she moved. I smiled, feeling a mix of nostalgia and happiness. Seeing her so excited made me forget, even for a moment, all the complications of my life.

We ordered our breakfast, and I made sure to get her the giant stack of pancakes she loved. The waitress brought them out with a playful wink, saying, "These are the birthday pancakes!" Claire's face lit up with delight, and she dug in with gusto. I watched her with a contented smile, feeling a warmth spread through me.

After breakfast, we headed back home. The day seemed to drift by peacefully. Claire played with her toys while I tidied up the house. The soft hum of the vacuum cleaner and the occasional giggle from Claire made the house feel like a warm, safe haven. I was lost in thought, thinking about how much had changed in the past few weeks—my discoveries about my family, my renewed connection with my dad, and just the complexities of my life.

As I was putting away the vacuum, I heard a strange noise coming from the garage. It was a muffled thud, followed by a scraping sound. My heart skipped a beat. We hadn't had any issues with the garage lately, but the noise set my nerves on edge.

"Claire, stay here and watch your show," I called out as I grabbed a frying pan from the kitchen. It wasn't the most conventional weapon, but it would do in a pinch. I took a deep breath and headed toward the garage, trying to stay as calm as possible.

When I flicked on the garage light, the room was flooded with light, and I was momentarily blinded by the brightness. As my eyes adjusted, I saw a gathering of familiar faces. The room erupted in cheers. "Surprise!"

I stood there, stunned, as I took in the scene before me. Josh, Callie, Carter, his family, Kiya, baby Christian, Elanor, and even my dad were there. My mouth fell open, and I could barely process what I was seeing. The garage had been transformed into a party space, complete with decorations, balloons, and a large banner that read "Happy Birthday Caitlyn & Claire!"

Callie stepped forward, her face lit up with a triumphant smile. "Surprise! We've been planning this for weeks."

"How? When?" I managed to stammer, still in shock. "How did you pull this off?"

Callie grinned and nudged Carter. "Thank Carter too. He's been a huge help."

Carter walked over and wrapped me in a warm hug. "Happy birthday, Caitlyn. I'm so glad we could do this for you."

I glanced around, taking in all the familiar faces and the effort that had clearly gone into the party. My dad approached and gave me a heartfelt hug. "It's good to see you, Caitlyn. I'm glad we could be here for your special day."

I felt a lump in my throat as I looked around at everyone. My dad and Carter's mom were talking to each other, exchanging smiles and laughter. I saw Elanor holding baby Christian, her eyes twinkling with pride. The sight of my grandmother holding my half-brother was a poignant reminder of the connections that bound us all together.

Claire, now curious about the commotion, wandered into the garage. Her eyes widened in amazement at the colorful decorations and the crowd of people. Callie immediately went over to her, bending down to her level. "Happy birthday, Claire! Look at all the fun stuff we have for you."

Claire's face broke into a wide grin. "Thank you!" She clutched her stuffed bunny tightly and looked around in awe.

As the party continued, I took a moment to appreciate the efforts everyone had made. I noticed Carter standing off to the side, watching me with a soft, affectionate smile. I walked over and took his hand, feeling the warmth of his touch.

"I'm really grateful for all this," I said, looking into his eyes. "Thank you for making it so special."

Carter leaned in and kissed me gently. "I'm just glad to see you happy. And I'm sorry that your mom couldn't make it. I know how much she wanted to be here."

I squeezed his hand, trying to keep my emotions in check. "It's okay. I appreciate everything you've done."

Callie reappeared with Claire in tow. "I'm going to go get Claire some snacks," she said with a wink. "I'll be back in a bit."

As the party continued, the atmosphere was filled with laughter and music. We ate, danced, and celebrated the day. The joy of being surrounded by loved ones was overwhelming. Callie, ever the prankster, had a surprise of her own.

"Okay, Caitlyn, I have one more surprise for you," she announced, her eyes gleaming mischievously. "Blindfold time!"

I playfully protested, but Callie insisted, and I let her tie the blindfold around my eyes. "Don't peek!" she warned as she guided me to a new location.

I could hear footsteps and muffled voices around me. The excitement in the air was evident. Then, I felt a gentle touch on my arms. I took a deep breath, wondering what was coming next.

Callie removed the blindfold, and as my eyes adjusted, I saw my mom standing in front of me, holding a gift. Her face was glowing, and she looked beautiful. The sight of her brought tears to my eyes. I have been praying to be able to see my mom the way I use to see her again.

"Mom?" I whispered, my voice trembling. "You're here."

She stepped forward and enveloped me in a warm hug. "Happy birthday, Caitlyn. I'm so sorry I couldn't be here earlier, but I made it."

I clutched her tightly, feeling the weight of everything we'd been through melt away. "Thank you. It means so much to me."

She handed me the gift box, and I opened it slowly. Inside was a small puppy, its eyes shining with curiosity. My heart ached with joy. "I know how hard it was when Cookie passed away," she said softly. "I wanted to give you another friend."

I hugged my mom again, my tears mixing with her smile. "I can't thank you enough. This is exactly what I needed." I said as I looked down at the dog. Spitting image of how cookie looked.

The party continued with renewed energy. My mom mingled with everyone, reconnecting with old friends and making new memories. I saw her chatting with my dad and Carter's mom, sharing stories and laughter.

As the night wore on, I gathered everyone for a final toast. The room quieted as I took a deep breath, feeling a wave of emotion.

"I want to thank everyone for being here today," I began, my voice steady but emotional. "Today is special not just because of the birthdays, but because of all of you. Each of you holds a special place in my heart, and I'm grateful for your love and support."

I glanced around at all the familiar faces—Callie, Carter, Josh, Kiya, Elanor, my dad, and everyone else who had come together to celebrate with us.

The warmth of their presence filled me with a deep sense of belonging and joy. I took one last look at Claire, who was happily playing with our new puppy, and then at my mother, who was laughing with the others.

"And I'm thankful for today," I continued, "because it reminds me that, despite everything, I'm surrounded by people who care about me and who make me feel special. I cherish these moments, and I'm reminded that life is precious and full of love."

I paused for a moment, letting the weight of my words settle. The room was filled with a soft, reflective silence as everyone absorbed the sentiment.

"I love you all."

The room erupted in applause and cheers. The words hung in the air, resonating with the essence of what we had all come together to celebrate. The party continued, filled with joy, laughter, and the deep connection that had brought us all together.

And as I looked around at the faces of those I loved, I felt a sense of peace. This was more than a birthday celebration—it was a testament to the resilience of family, the power of forgiveness, and the beauty of shared moments.

I always use to think I was put on this earth just to endure pain. I thought because I was born, I had to pay. Pay for my mother's mistakes, pay for my father's wrong doing. But now, because I was born, I look forward to the future. I look forward to what will come next. There is so much more ahead for me, so much in store.

Now that I'm alive.

# BECAUSE I WAS BORN
Alycia Jones

# Now That I'm Alive: The Story Continues

I stared at my watch, pacing back and forth. Ugh, where is he? The evening breeze tugged at the hem of my dress, reminding me of the chill in the air, but my thoughts were too tangled up in anticipation to care. Every minute that passed felt like an hour, my excitement and anxiety blending into a confusing mix of emotions.

I glanced at the road again, hoping to see his car pulling up. My heart raced at the thought of finally being in his arms again. It had been way too long, and I could hardly wait to feel his embrace, to melt into the comfort of his presence. I bit my lip, imagining the warmth of his body, the way his eyes would light up when he saw me. The memories of our last night together played in my mind, making my pulse quicken even more.

I sighed, trying to calm myself down. He'll be here any minute, I told myself, but it didn't stop the flutter in my chest. I wanted to see him, to tell him everything. My life had taken so many twists and turns, and he was the one constant that kept me grounded. The one person who made everything feel right, no matter how crazy things got.

The sound of an approaching engine made me look up. My heart skipped a beat as I saw headlights in the distance, getting closer and closer. This is it, I thought, feeling a smile tug at my lips. I stepped forward, my hands trembling with anticipation.

The car came to a stop, and the door swung open. I held my breath, my eyes fixed on the figure stepping out. He was finally here. My heart swelled with love as I watched him move toward me, his familiar silhouette making me feel like everything was going to be okay.

He looked up, and our eyes met. A grin spread across his face, that same boyish smile that made my knees weak. "Hey, babe," he said, his voice soft yet electrifying.

"Quinn!" I breathed, rushing forward into his arms. He caught me, lifting me off the ground as I wrapped my arms around his neck. Our lips met in a kiss that sent a jolt of electricity through my entire body.

When we finally pulled away, I gazed into his eyes, my heart still racing. "I've missed you so much," I whispered, my fingers tracing the line of his jaw.

"I missed you too, babe,"

# About the Author

**Alycia Jones** was born and raised in North Miami Beach, Florida. Her writing is deeply rooted in her feelings, serving as a powerful outlet for self-expression. When she's not writing, Alycia enjoys singing and playing the piano, further channeling her creativity through music. She believes that both writing and music allow her to connect with others on a profound level. Alycia is currently working on more projects, so stay tuned!

**You can connect with me on:**

f https://www.facebook.com/alycia.jones.771

Made in the USA
Columbia, SC
02 November 2024

933547fd-a866-4e33-a687-fd30082038beR01